ANN JACOBS

Men in Motion

ELLORA'S CAVE
ROMANTICA® PUBLISHING

HOT IN THE CLUTCH

After twenty years in the NFL, Dave Delaney's playing days are over and he's back home in Hedgecock, Texas, coaching football at his old high school. He's tired of meaningless sex and his empty lifestyle. Dave is ready for change and sets his sights on the girl who got away.

Diane Connors is attracted in a big way, but Dave is used to being chased by groupies almost young enough to be his daughters. He's still a chick magnet with a wild reputation, and she's gun-shy after escaping a miserable marriage with a bully — another local jock.

Thing is, neither of them can forget what might have been.

COACH ME

Master me, thinks Susan Anderson when she finally lays eyes on Colin Zanardi, former NFL MVP and now coach of the Savannah Rebels. He is only in town for a few days, but he's the Dom she's been dreaming of, yearning for. She just has to convince him to play with her, show him how submissive and obedient she is, and demonstrate just what she can do for that gorgeous body of his.

It's been a long time since Colin has played with a true submissive. Susan is eager to be dominated. By him. He's the perfect Master to tame her, and settling down this firecracker is a challenge Colin can't resist. He can think of so many things he wants to use on her — a sex swing, a spiderweb, a roomful of sex toys.

He'll play her scene — tie her, blindfold her, order her to pleasure him — for their mutual satisfaction. Colin is more than ready to turn this hometown party girl into his own private sex slave.

An Ellora's Cave Romantica Publication

www.ellorascave.com

Men in Motion

MEN IN MOTION
Ann Jacobs

&

HOT IN THE CLUCH
~9~

COACH ME
~97~

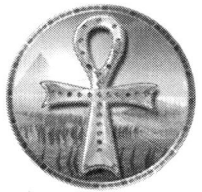

HOT IN THE CLUTCH

ଊଠ

Trademarks Acknowledgement

The author acknowledges the trademarked status and trademark owners of the following wordmarks mentioned in this work of fiction:

737: The Boeing Company

Coke: The Coca Cola Company

Escalade: General Motors Corporation

FedEx: FedEx Corporation

Field Turf: Tarkett Sports, A Tarkett Company

Jacuzzi: Jacuzzi, Inc.

Jenn-Air: Maytag Corporation

NFL, NFL Network: NFL Enterprises LLC

Pinot Noir: Williams Selyem Winery, Sonoma, California

Prestige Rose: Taittinger, Reims, France

Reeboks: Reebok International Limited

Super Bowl: National Football League unincorporated association

Tiffany's: Tiffany & Co.

Viagra: Pfizer, Inc.

Author's Notes and Glossary

ઌ

I'm a rabid football fan, or rather a rabid fan of several generations of quarterbacks I've watched play on TV and in person. This fandom caused me to come up with an idea for the Gridiron Lovers, a series of erotic romances about four star quarterbacks who just happened to have grown up in the same small west Texas town and who went on to fame and fortune as professionals. All of these guys and their teams are fictional, and any resemblance to an actual NFL player or team past or present is purely coincidental.

The four books' titles apparently need some explanation for readers who haven't been watching games every fall since…well, for quite a few years. Suffice it to say, I've watched every Super Bowl since number three, when Broadway Joe Namath came through on his guarantee of a win for the New York Jets. I was just a baby then (wink-wink).

So here we go. Mind you, these definitions may not all be technically correct, since they're based on my personal observations and comments I've digested from the media personalities who call the games on TV every Sunday from August through December and early January. Take a minute and read these pages first, or as my Aussie editor says, you may become totally confused.

Naked Bootleg. This is a play where the quarterback takes the snap, fakes a handoff to a running back but keeps the ball. He runs the opposite direction from the runner without a lineman protecting him—this makes the bootleg "naked"—and either passes to a receiver downfield or runs downfield himself. I thought it was a great play for Bobby Anthony to make during his first NFL appearance, as well as a sexy-sounding title for the first Gridiron Lovers book.

Forward Pass. The quarterback drops back from the line of scrimmage and throws the ball forward to an eligible receiver downfield. Eligible receivers, I think, are the backs, tight ends and wide receivers. Keith Connors is a master of the forward pass on the field, but he's pretty hot in the bedroom, as well.

Clutch, as in *Hot in the Clutch*. A player, usually a quarterback, who's especially good at coming through with points when the team needs them most. Dave Delaney's career is almost over, but he can still be counted on for a great play in the clutch, whether it's on the field or in a woman's bed.

Coach, as in *Coach Me*. The masterminds of the game, often former players great or average. Each team has several coaches, with the "head coach" in charge of it all. Colin Zanardi's playing days are over, but he's still in the game, not only with his team but also with the hottest of the local ladies.

Now for the glossary, which I'm putting in alphabetical order so you can refer to it as needed while you read:

Athletic waivers: a certain number of exceptions a college coach can use to recruit top athletes who don't meet minimum academic standards for the institution which are determined by a combination of high school grades and standardized test scores.

Audible: when the quarterback calls out a change of the play at the line of scrimmage.

Block: what linemen do to keep defensive players away from the quarterback, as in "throw a block" or "miss a block".

Center: the player on the offensive line who snaps the ball to the quarterback when he's "under center" or "in the shotgun".

Clipboard: the object that all backup quarterbacks almost always have in their hands while standing on the sidelines; a backup quarterback's assignment, as in "carry the clipboard".

Depth chart: a chart that shows each player's status at his position—starter, second string, third string, etc.

Double coverage: two defensive players are covering (chasing) one potential receiver for the offense at the same time.

Field position: the spot on the hundred-yard field where the ball is spotted—the closer to the defense's goal, the better the field position is for the offense.

First down: when the offense starts a series or moves ten yards down the field toward the opponent's goal—can be a longer or shorter distance if penalties are involved—and is then given four more tries to make another ten yards or a touchdown, or kick the ball away.

Fumble: when the football gets loose from whatever player had it in his hands and is fair game for any player, either offensive or defensive, to pick up and claim—called a fumble recovery.

Groupie: a woman who's obsessed with professional athletes and wants any athlete, but preferably a star, for a day or night's fun and games.

Handoff: when the quarterback takes the snap from the center and immediately hands it to a running back.

Huddle: a gathering of the entire offense around the quarterback, who gives them the play the coach has sent from the sideline or via a speaker in the quarterback's helmet.

Interception: when an opposing player catches a pass, thereby causing the defense to get the ball.

Linebackers: defensive players who often break through the offensive line and go after the quarterback (there are three of them in some defenses, four in others); they also break up pass plays downfield by stopping the receivers who are trying to catch passes and/or get additional yards after catching the ball.

Line of scrimmage: the point on the football field where the ball is placed.

Nose tackle: a defensive player who lines up in front of the center, usually a huge beast of a man who opens up holes in the offense so other defensive players can get to the quarterback (Note: this assumes the defense is what's called a three-four where the nose tackle and two defensive ends line up in front, with four linebackers behind them—the setup is different, although I can't explain how, if the defense is a so-called four-three with two tackles and two defensive ends in front and three linebackers behind them).

Penalty: a misdeed on the part of an offensive or defensive player that causes the team to be penalized from five to fifteen yards, and sometimes—in the case of a penalty on the defense—to create an automatic first down for the offense. Some of the reasons penalties are imposed are for holding, roughing the passer, unnecessary roughness, illegal motion before the ball is snapped, extra man on the field, or illegal formation.

Pick-six: an interception that the defensive player runs back for a touchdown.

Punt: kick on fourth down, so the opposing team will get the ball as far as possible downfield; *punter:* the player who kicks punts.

Receiver, or wide receiver: an offensive player whose main function is to catch passes from the quarterback.

Running back: offensive player who takes handoffs from the quarterback and runs the ball, or who catches short passes "out of the backfield" and then runs for yardage.

Sack: when a defensive player gets to the quarterback before he passes the ball and throws him to the ground.

Scout team: a team of non-starting players who study and then try to duplicate the plays of an opposing team while the first team practices against them during the week before the actual game (the backup quarterback usually runs the scout team, although sometimes that job goes to the third-string guy).

Shotgun: a formation where the quarterback stands a good distance back from the center to take the snap.

Snap: the movement of the ball from the center to the quarterback.

Taking a knee: when the quarterback takes the snap and goes down on one knee instead of initiating a play as the time is winding down to zero at halftime or at the end of a game.

Three-and-out: an expression that describes an offensive series where the offense goes three snaps without getting a first down.

Tight end: offensive players who generally line up at the ends of the offensive line (if there are two of them in for the play) and who block as well as catch passes.

Turnover: the offense gives the ball to the other team because of a fumble or interception rather than after three-and-out or a touchdown.

I hope you all enjoy this series as much as I've loved putting it together. *Naked Bootleg* started it all, and it's the only book that takes place during football season—so you won't see a lot of actual playing—at least on the field—in the stories that follow. Kick back now and enjoy *Hot in the Clutch*, the story of how a former MVP's career ends and his new life begins.

Prologue

∽

As two teammates helped him limp off the field, Dave Delaney finally understood why Rosa had wanted him to retire. His right knee—the one the surgeons had put back together two years ago—hurt like hell. Yeah, he'd managed to get another shot at the Lombardi Trophy, but at what cost?

Lying on a stretcher on the sideline with worried-looking doctors and trainers examining him as if he were a side of beef was no damn fun. Neither was listening to hordes of Maulers fans screaming over his carcass like forty thousand predators ripe for the kill, or the smaller group of Rebels fans yelling at him to get up and back into the game.

"You're done, Delaney," the doc said, his tone funereal.

What the fuck? After today Dave's career was history, but he'd go out like a man, not a sniveling coward. "Like hell. Tape it up good and tight and put my brace on." Bad as he hated wearing the clumsy device he'd had fitted after his first knee surgery, it was the only way he was going to be able to walk back on the field.

"You'll hurt yourself worse."

"No matter. I'll survive until we win this game. Then I'm done."

It wasn't as though Coach had anybody else to put in. The Rebels' emergency quarterback was just that—an emergency waiting to happen. Dave had to go back in or they might as well forfeit the Super Bowl. He winced at the pressure the trainer applied while taping his swollen knee. Head Coach Colin Zanardi stood over Dave, a worried look on his face. "You gonna make it, Dave?"

"I'll be okay. No need to panic." Of course that was wishful thinking. The likelihood was that the Rebels' current lead wasn't going to last, especially not with him off his game. He'd lie to Coach but not to himself. Not particularly mobile in the best of times, Dave figured he'd be a statue out there now, the way he was hurting. A sitting duck waiting to be shot down. "Just have the guys protect me better than they did on that last play."

"They'll do their best."

Dave hoped so. He also hoped his linemen would put a hurting on the Maulers linebacker who'd laid the late hit on him. Bastard deserved to feel more than the five-figure fine the league would probably levy after reviewing the game tape.

This was it. His last football game. He couldn't fool himself anymore. The throbbing in his knee told him as certainly as the sober look in the doc's eye and the reservation in the coach's. A win would be sweet, but he could deal with an honest loss. It smarted to think he might be going out a loser because some asshole Maulers defender wouldn't play by the rules.

* * * * *

Back home in Hedgecock, Texas, Diane Connors stretched out on the couch, watching her younger brother Keith march his Maulers team up and down the field. Dylan, her son, lay sprawled on the rug in front of her, his eyes glued to the TV.

Diane knew Dave Delaney, the Savannah Rebels quarterback, from way back. Despite being past forty years old, Dave was holding on to a lead in the tight game. Or at least he had been until a minute ago when two Maulers defenders turned him into the filling for a human sandwich. Without his helmet, Dave looked a lot like she remembered from long ago. Older now, obviously, he still had the wavy black hair and electric blue eyes that proclaimed his Black Irish ancestry. Pain registered on that handsome face as two of his teammates helped him off the field.

Why was he still punishing himself? Diane shuddered as she watched the coach, a doctor and a trainer on the sideline looking at Dave's right knee. If she wasn't mistaken, that was the same knee he'd had surgery on a couple of seasons ago.

"Hey, Mom, Uncle Keith just threw for a touchdown." Dylan sat up, shot her a frustrated look. "Why couldn't we go to the game?"

"Because I said so." Diane wished Keith hadn't sent them tickets, sort of an apology for having contacted her last fall about a nanny for his motherless baby when they hadn't spoken for years before that. He'd been well-intentioned, for sure, only he hadn't thought about how the tickets weren't even half the cost of attending the game. She wasn't about to accept charity from Keith—he hadn't put her in the financial straits she'd been in since she'd let Frank talk her into buying a struggling rodeo stock operation that eventually went belly-up. "It costs a fortune to get from here to New Orleans—not to mention we'd have had to stay in a hotel and pay somebody to look after the animals. If your uncle wants to see us, he can come here."

She turned back to the screen, registered that the Maulers had tied the score—and that Dave was standing on the sideline now, helmet in hand. Tall, rangy-looking even in pads, he still was a chick magnet just as he'd been in high school. Briefly she wondered if he knew his old girlfriend, Edie, had died last fall.

Probably not. Dave had walked away from Edie when he left for college, and as far as Diane knew, he'd never looked back. On the few occasions he'd come to Hedgecock, he'd stayed briefly to visit his grandma and an elderly aunt. The last time, two years ago when he'd come for his grandma's funeral, he'd brought along his country-singing-star wife and their two kids, not too long before a very public split-up. Maybe he'd come back here after he retired, but Diane doubted it.

She shot one last glance at the screen and saw Dave limping onto the field, a broken gladiator refusing to give up the fight.

"Looks like Delaney's hurt pretty bad." Dylan reached into the popcorn bowl, found it empty. "Hey, do we have any more popcorn, Mom?"

"There's another bag on the counter. You can microwave it during the commercial."

Dylan shot her a surprised look, probably because he thought she'd volunteer to go make another bag. But she hadn't wanted to see the end of a game this much since she was in high school and Dave was throwing passes right here in Hedgecock.

She must be losing her mind! Squinting a little at the screen, she picked out the Maulers guy who'd put that vicious hit on Dave, clenched her fists. *Dirty bastard.* It looked like he could hardly wait to lay a hurt on somebody again.

The huge, menacing hulk reminded her of her ex-husband and the fact he'd been thrown off the Hedgecock High team years ago because he took pleasure in hurting opponents. The guy grappling now with a Rebels offensive tackle might have been better off working off his aggression by taking up bull riding the way Frank had. She'd like to see Keith's teammate taking on an opponent that outweighed him by a thousand pounds or more and was at least twice as mean.

Dave handed off the ball before the hulk got to him, but he got tackled anyhow. Miraculously he heaved himself up off the ground and lined up in shotgun, completing a short pass before getting knocked down again. This time the referee called the hulk for a personal foul—unnecessary roughness. That gave the Rebels a first down.

Just looking at that hurt. Diane had watched a lot of football games in her life, and she'd never seen such patently dirty play. Good thing she and her brother weren't close or she'd have felt bad for praying his team would lose. Why did the referees let the Maulers' defense get by with flagrant violations of the rules?

"Mom, would you please fix the popcorn? I don't want to miss any of the game." Dylan held up his empty bowl.

Diane wasn't sure she wanted to watch any more. She wasn't at all certain she wanted Dylan to watch the carnage, either. She hated that he seemed to relish the violence—just as Frank always had. "Sure. Do you want another Coke?"

"Yeah. Hey, see that guy McRae on Uncle Keith's team? He's putting a real hurting on Delaney."

Diane didn't want to watch some bully trying to hurt the long-ago heartthrob of her own high school. She sighed, turned back toward the kitchen. "I think the idea is to keep the quarterback from passing, not grind him into the turf after he's already thrown the ball. I hope you don't think unnecessary violence is cool."

"Nah. It's sure likely to help Uncle Keith's team win, though. The Rebels' backup quarterback has never thrown an NFL pass." Dylan paused, glanced over at her. "You knew Delaney when you were a kid, didn't you?"

"Uh-huh. He used to date Edie when we all were in high school."

Dylan grinned. "Then I won't cheer for McRae to knock ol' Dave out of the game."

"Okay. I'm sure he'd appreciate that."

By the time she got back to the TV, the two-minute warning had sounded. The Maulers had tied the score. They had the ball and were moving close to field-goal range.

Dylan muttered a brief thanks and stuffed his mouth with popcorn, never taking his gaze from the screen. He watched the screen with what looked like morbid glee while his uncle moved the ball downfield, but Diane couldn't help concentrating on the sideline when the cameras panned that way. It tore at her, seeing the pain and disappointment in

Dave's expression as he sat, his face pale beneath normally swarthy skin, plastic bags of ice packed around his knee.

She'd rather remember Dave the way he'd looked after his last high school victory. Totally pumped, that engaging smile warming everybody around him as he found and kissed every one of the cheerleaders, Diane included. Seeing him again, even through the electronic magic of TV, made her remember his soft lips and hard body and the shiver of desire his touch had sent coursing through her veins.

Of course, back then he'd belonged to her best friend Edie. She could think about what might have been, but the truth was that Frank Granger had claimed Diane early her freshman year and they'd stuck together even after he'd graduated two years before her. Now, twenty-some-odd years later, Edie and Frank were gone. She and Dave had managed to survive in their respective worlds, miles apart.

Even so, she hated seeing him this way now, apparently torn up not just on the outside but inside, too. And it hurt her, knowing his marriage had broken up and that he might be all alone with the injury she sensed was serious. When the game ended a few minutes later after a Maulers field goal for the win, Diane sensed this gridiron warrior had played pro football for the last time. Though she told herself she was fantasizing, she wondered again if he might come back to Hedgecock not just for the reunion this spring, but to stay. After all, his grandma had left him her place down the road, and as far as she knew, he hadn't made any attempt to sell it.

If he did, their paths might cross again.

Chapter One
Hedgecock, Texas, a few weeks later

ಬಿ

It turned out that Keith did come to see them—in a roundabout way. He came back to Hedgecock to get married. Diane was still in a bit of a shock over it. That nanny her brother had needed turned out to be none other than Tina Black, Edie's daughter. And they'd come back to Hedgecock to tie the knot.

Diane felt good that she'd encouraged Keith to hire Tina, but she couldn't help feeling guilty that she hadn't stuck by Edie after she'd married Edgar Garcia. The man had always given her the creeps—he was as much a bully as Frank but a sexual predator to boot. Edie had been the sort of woman who needed a man—any man—to take care of her, and old Edgar had taken advantage.

If Diane had known at the time what Edgar was doing to Tina...but she hadn't. It didn't matter now because Tina seemed crazy in love with Keith and a loving stepmom toward his year-old son.

Smiling, Diane turned to her friend Melanie Tate, who was hosting the reception for Keith and Tina. Good thing, because the Tate house was the only place in the county big enough to hold most of Hedgecock County's population plus fifty or so of Keith's Maulers teammates, coaches and front-office people who'd come for the wedding. Even their mother had come from Colorado, as much as she hated everything about Hedgecock. She'd be taking Keith's son home for a visit while Keith and Tina jetted off to Hawaii for their honeymoon.

"They make a nice couple. Guess I was right after all, sending Tina to Memphis after Edie died and Garcia started stalking her." Mel smiled at Diane. "Tina and Keith seem so right for each other."

"Yeah. They do. Makes me feel old, though, seeing my baby brother marrying my best friend's little girl."

"Uh-huh. We're all pushing middle age." Mel glanced across the room at her new husband Cal Tate and grinned. "I've found the best cure for feeling old is falling back in love. You ought to try it. Maybe make a play for Dave. If I remember right, you were pretty starry-eyed over him way back when."

Diane glanced across the room at the subject of Mel's teasing. Even using forearm crutches and walking with a limp, the guy was still incredibly hot, with that brooding Black Irish look about him. Well over six feet tall, though a bit shorter than Keith or Bobby, he had a rough-edged look she imagined had intimidated a lot of opponents over the years. "He and Edie were joined at the hip until he left for college. I didn't have a chance." She wasn't sure she'd have wanted one, deep down, because even Edie had always said the star quarterback was too wild for any girl to tame.

"Not to mention that Frank had laid his claim on you." Mel's smile faded, and she slapped a hand over her mouth. "I shouldn't have said that."

"It's okay. I've had plenty of time to regret Frank Granger and everything about him. Other than Dylan, of course. It's a good thing for my son that he hardly ever reminds me of his rotten father." Diane glanced back over at Dave then turned to Mel. "You know, if Tina were a couple of years older, she could have been Dave's daughter."

Mel shook her head. "Dave was too smart to have let that happen. He had things to prove, places to go. Women to seduce, if what I've heard is true."

"Yeah." For a minute Diane let herself imagine how different her life could have been if she'd been with Dave instead of Frank, who'd bullied her into marrying him more than twenty years ago when she'd been too young and foolish to be cautious of his possessiveness and evil temper. She took in Dave's studied bad-boy pose, his tousled black hair, his electric blue gaze lazily perusing the scene. She wished for a minute that he'd chosen her, not her best friend, to take under the bleachers for those after-game celebrations under the west Texas moon. If he had, she might have learned sex was fun, not a painful necessity to maintain some semblance of peace with Frank. "I wonder why Dave's wife left him."

"From what Bobby told me, they were both into partying, and not necessarily with each other. Of course that's just what he's heard from other players. It's too bad. They've got two kids, a boy and a girl who're with their mom in California. Nice-looking kids. Remember, he brought them with him a few years ago when he came home for his grandma's funeral."

"Yeah. It is too bad. For the kids, at least." Diane thought of Dylan, who despite his interest in watching his uncle play pro ball on TV, usually preferred to escape into his books. She knew their relationship had been strained since she'd tossed Frank off the ranch nearly five years ago, though Dylan had witnessed Frank hitting her more than once. She hadn't had much choice in the matter after Frank had used his fists and broken her collarbone when she'd tried to pull him off Dylan. Up until the day he died, she'd been afraid for Dylan as well as herself. "I'd bet good money that Dave never hurt any of them."

She couldn't imagine him being anything but great with his own kids. Earlier in the week she'd seen him out on the high school field, tossing footballs with kids way too young for him to be recruiting for his team. His dog, a sooty gray standard poodle, retrieved balls for him when the boys threw them out of his reach. Diane hadn't been able to resist stopping to watch for a minute, wondering if he'd be as patient and gentle with a woman as he seemed to be with the children. He laughed when he missed catching a ball thrown right at him, shrugged as though it didn't matter that he had to lean on a crutch to keep his balance.

When he'd called the boys to him, the dog had trotted along, too. He'd bent to stroke her curly topknot then looked Diane's way. For a few seconds their gazes had met, and she'd felt recognition as well as a sexual heat that made her cheeks burn. Embarrassed, she'd put her truck in gear and pulled away.

Now she sensed he was looking at her and glanced his way. She read sadness in his brooding expression, wondering if he missed his family, wished things had been different.

She recognized the perfect drape of his dark suit that practically screamed "custom tailored", and she'd have bet money that the ivory silk shirt he wore open at the collar bore some pricey designer label. Those clothes came from Dave's other life, reminding Diane that he might have come back, but he wasn't the same boy who'd left so long ago. "I wonder how long he's going to stay."

"For a while, I imagine. He's taking over for Coach Williams next week, coaching the high school football team. If you're still attracted to the guy, you should go after him. You know you would have back in the day if it hadn't been for Edie."

Had Diane been that transparent? "I'd have never done anything to hurt Edie." Petite, pretty and easily led, Edie had always seemed to need an extra dose of protection from her friends since she'd never gotten it from her lovers. Diane wondered if Dave had even thought about the tears her best friend had shed when he'd walked away from her and Hedgecock toward a future that hadn't included nurturing a high school romance.

Maybe…

No. Although Diane had always been a lot stronger than Edie, that didn't mean she was strong enough to weather falling for the bad boy of her generation now, after her own marriage had shattered. Her experience with Frank had left her brittle and pretty much expecting the worst from members of the male persuasion.

On the other hand, she might not be averse to having a fast fling with Dave, for old time's sake. She bit her lip, startled at the unexpected thought. She was a mom, for heaven's sake. And yet...she still had all the female hormones. Her memories of sex with Frank were more or less a waking nightmare but maybe, with the right partner, she might find gettin' it on was fun.

And with it being a fling, it didn't have to involve Dylan or her responsibilities toward him. She wasn't about to let a here-today-gone-tomorrow male role model into his life, that was for certain. But for herself...she tried to push down the reaction of her body to such a thought. If Mel's knowing grin was any indication, she wasn't successful.

Ah, hell, forty was damn young to give up on sex, even for a woman who no longer believed in love. Whatever else he might be, Dave Delaney was one tasty-looking hunk, at least to Diane's deprived eyes.

* * * * *

Keith Connors was nothing if not a lucky fucking bastard.

Dave shifted to take pressure off his knee and leaned against the wall, watching the guy who'd beaten him in the Super Bowl last month celebrating his wedding—to Tina Black. Ironic, Connors marrying the pretty daughter of one of Dave's own old high school lovers.

He and Keith had been nodding acquaintances since Dave was a teenager and Keith an annoying snot-nosed kid. The best man, a fresh-faced rookie named Bobby Anthony, quarterbacked the Orlando team Dave owned a piece of. By the time Bobby had been pestering a teenaged Keith, Dave had been long gone, enjoying the best seasons of his career. Bobby, a big, gangly kid with huge hands and feet, seemed happy as a clam, showing off the sexy cheerleader he'd married a few months ago.

The reminders of his knee and his retired status in the face of Keith's having beaten him in the Super Bowl and Bobby's freshness in the game almost had him escaping as soon as Connors got hitched. Unfortunately Rosa, his ex, had always insisted it was rude for guests to leave events like this too soon. So he'd stayed and tried not to feel jealous because his career was over while Keith and Bobby had years to anticipate as players.

He'd wolfed down a dozen or so fancy girl-sized sandwiches, some meatballs and a big chunk of wedding cake, made small talk with old acquaintances. And he'd just fended off a blatant advance from Susan Anderson, a classmate who apparently still would fuck any guy she could talk into unzipping his pants.

He'd been careful not only to give Susan a friendly "no thanks" but also to take it easy on the high-priced champagne he doubted many Hedgecock locals had ever seen before. After all, he didn't want the locals seeing their new football coach womanizing and slugging down the bubbly as if there were no tomorrow. Particularly since his penchant for partying used to be one of the media's favorite topics when he was riding high, winning playoff spots nearly every year.

Damn. He had to squash the self-pity, so he focused on something that made him feel better. Although it still shocked him, he was actually looking forward to following old Coach Williams as coach at the high school where he'd once been a star. Yeah, it was a far cry from the NFL, but a man had to have something to occupy his days, and Dave hadn't been able to picture himself doing color commentary on TV for games he no longer could play.

A month ago he wouldn't have given a shit, but somehow…

Losing everything—Rosa and his children, his career, a decent chunk of the money and things he'd amassed over the years—had eventually made Dave realize he wasn't the same smartass kid he'd been when he left Hedgecock twenty-four years ago for college, fame and fortune.

When he'd found out Keith was marrying Edie's daughter, that had been a shock. But it had floored him to learn Edie had passed away. She'd been his age, maybe a little younger. That underscored how life was way too short. Maybe his having to retire wasn't such a bad thing. At least he had thirty or forty years of living to look forward to, the Lord willing. Time to focus on more important things.

As if his mind had been cued by the thought, Dave's gaze strayed to the opposite side of the room where Diane, Keith's sister, was talking with Mel Tate. He'd heard she'd divorced Frank Granger, hoped she'd gone back to Connors. It kind of surprised him to have that reaction. The surge of attraction he'd felt for her back in high school came back today, even stronger.

She still had that cool, collected look about her, and time hadn't done anything to make her look any less hot. He liked the way she wore her blonde hair down today instead of in the ponytail he remembered, imagined it would feel like silk in his hands.

Wearing a simple blue dress almost the color of her eyes, she looked even prettier than he remembered her. He'd had the hots for her back then but kept his distance, though her cool blonde beauty had made him wonder if she'd be as hot in bed as she was calm and collected in school. She'd been joined at the hip with Frank Granger, one mean SOB if Dave ever met one—and the three-hundred-pound bully had made mincemeat of more than one underclassman who'd tried to hit on Diane.

Somebody ought to have clued her in on what a creep she was dating. Somebody probably had, but Diane had seemed to like the fact that Frank was so possessive—and Frank apparently had reserved his physical violence back then for other guys. From what he'd heard from Keith when they spoke a couple of days ago, Frank had graduated from verbal to physical abuse pretty soon after they'd married against their mom's wishes, but Diane had been too proud to let anybody know until he started in on Dylan.

The bastard. When Dave heard Granger had gotten killed a while back while riding a bull at some rodeo up in Denver, he'd figured uncharitably that Frank had finally got his comeuppance. He felt even more so now that he knew what a hell the creep had made of Diane's life.

He'd squelched the urge to pursue Diane years ago. He wouldn't do it again. Straightening up and making his way around a dwindling crowd, he stopped when he reached Diane and Mel. "Congratulations on marrying off your pest of a brother, Diane."

Both women laughed, as though they recalled how Dave had always groused about Keith following him around all the time way back when. "I was sorry to hear the pest got the best of you in the Super Bowl," Mel said. "But we're all glad you've come back home."

"Yes. We were wondering if we'd ever find a good replacement for Coach Williams. Now we have." Diane paused then smiled up at him. "I saw you playing on the field with some grade-school kids the other day. You're going to be a great coach. You are planning to stay awhile, aren't you?"

"I'm not sure but I'm giving it a shot. I've had Grandma's house remodeled and enlarged and so far I'm enjoying the peace and quiet out there. Daisy—my daughter's dog—seems to like the wide-open spaces, too, though she's spent all her life until now in big-city apartments."

"Has Daisy met any of our local cacti yet?" Mel asked. "Cal's and my Jack Russell terrier had to learn about their spines the hard way."

Dave grinned. "Not yet. She's awfully smart, and she seems to have a sixth sense about strange-looking plants that could stick her. Sort of like I remember cows and horses used to have enough sense to give a wide berth to cacti out in the pasture."

"How does Hedgecock seem to you now?"

"Weird, mainly because nothing much seems to have changed. As soon as my knee gets better, I want to get around and meet all the players' families. Right now, though, I have to baby it so it will heal." He might always have to favor it, or so the doctors said—but he intended to do whatever it took to get back his mobility.

They made small talk for a few minutes, with Dave wishing all the while that Mel would find something she needed to do so he could try putting a gentle hit on Diane. But she didn't.

Okay. He had time. Hedgecock being as small as it was, he'd likely run into her again within a day or so. Keith and Tina had already made their escape, and he'd had all he could take of small talk and the sound of clattering dishes in a nearby kitchen. "Speaking of knees, mine's telling me I've been standing for too long, so I'd better get on home and soak in the whirlpool tub. It was a nice wedding. I'm sure Keith and Tina will be very happy."

Diane laid her hand briefly on his shoulder. "Say hello to Daisy for me. She's quite the dog. I saw her playing catch with you and the boys."

"I will. See you later." As Dave made his way home he remembered Diane's comment about seeing Daisy on the high school field. She'd stopped and watched, though she'd bolted like a calf at branding time when she realized he'd seen her. She might very well be gun-shy but she wasn't oblivious to him. Meanwhile he'd go hang with his daughter's poodle. He'd brought her with him into exile, and she'd proven to be better company than a lot of humans.

* * * * *

31

Back home, Dave sat on Grandma's porch the way he'd taken to doing every day at sunset. Despite his need to get away from the reception for solitude, now it seemed too quiet. He realized he hadn't wanted to be alone as much as he'd desired to be *here*, sitting quietly *with* someone. With a woman, to be specific. Hell, seeing Diane was really playing with his head because he was already imagining her on this porch, sitting in a rocker, her bare feet tucked up underneath her, sipping wine while her hair fluttered along her shoulders. Maybe her sweater would be falling off one side, showing a bare collarbone he might stroke or kiss. Maybe he'd bring her onto his lap for some slow, easy lovemaking that would eventually get as hot and steady as that pumpjack, ticking off time like a metronome.

Yeah, it was too damn quiet out here all alone except for his cell phone and his dog and that slow-pumping oil well half obscured by a tumbledown fence. Keeping his legs straightened out in front of him, he sipped a Coke. If he was serious about going after Diane, and he thought he was, he'd better get a contractor out here to replace the fences and repair Grandma's rickety old barn. As he recalled, Diane used to love riding horseback, so he'd need someplace to keep a few if…

No need to count his blessings before they materialized. Dave concentrated on the pumpjack, followed its slow movement on the sparse horizon. Like Hedgecock, it moved at a snail's pace, much slower than the sometimes-frantic tempo of the NFL. Dave wondered how he might manage spending the rest of his life here, teaching kids to play the game he loved but could no longer play. He'd start finding out next week.

Closing his eyes, he tried to clear his mind, but he recognized the simmering tension that had dogged him since the reception and seeing Diane. He needed to get laid. No, it was more than that. Yeah, it had been almost two months since he'd made a shockingly young groupie's day by fucking her after the division championship game. But he'd awakened the next morning feeling more than a little ashamed of himself. He could have taken Susan Anderson home from the reception since she'd made her no-strings-attached fuck invitation loud and clear. But he hadn't wanted that, either. And though he could deny it, he knew damn well why.

He and Rosa had had an open marriage for nearly fifteen years. He'd had enough of that sort of relationship to last a lifetime. If he ever went for a woman again that way—as in something intended to be permanent and lasting—he'd do it the old-fashioned way, looking for fidelity and complete commitment for both of them. He wondered if Diane were that kind of woman, the faithful kind he was looking for.

He thought she would be, if she could trust any man after Frank. She certainly had stayed loyal to him through high school, though he'd already graduated. Dave considered what she'd been through, wondered if she'd ever heal enough to want a forever kind of love. She would if he had half the ability with women as media people used to credit him with. If she'd even give him a chance, considering his well-publicized sexual history, both truth and rumor.

Darkness was beginning to cloak the scene. A brilliant sunset crept down in the western sky. Dave whistled for Daisy and went inside, letting the rustic ambience of his grandma's living room with its rocking chairs and tinware geegaws on the hearth transport him to a time when he'd had everything to look forward to, when everything had been possible and nothing lay beyond his reach.

He'd wanted to keep this room the way he remembered it being since his mom dumped him on Grandma Delaney and never came back. He'd been just three years old at the time, but he'd never forgotten the sense of wonder he'd felt when he first saw Grandma's cast-iron piggy bank—the same one that sat smugly on the mantel, across from a collection of framed photos, including several of him in uniforms of pro teams he'd played for over the years.

The architect who'd designed the remodeling had tried to talk him out of keeping this room and the porch as they were, but Dave had insisted. He didn't give a damn that the old-fashioned room seemed out of synch with the rest of the house that he'd had enlarged and updated.

When Daisy laid her head on his knee, Dave scratched her topknot while he called Cathy and DJ for their weekly phone visit. "I miss you, too, guys. Maybe you can come out to Hedgecock for the summer."

He doubted Rosa would okay them coming to visit for more than the two weeks the judge had awarded him. Well, maybe she would, now that he no longer was playing pro ball. She might even take her new boyfriend along on her summer concert tour instead of dragging the kids with her on her tour bus. When Dave stripped down and crawled in bed after hanging up the phone, he closed his eyes and tried to clear his mind.

Faces flashed on the screen inside his head. Happy faces, sad ones, even Rosa's smug visage. Dave saw thirteen-year-old DJ tossing a football with one of the band guys, eleven-year-old Cathy looking lost and lonely without Daisy at her side. Trying to push down the nagging pain of things he currently didn't know how to change, he went back to the faces he'd seen at the wedding, attempting to distract himself.

Restless, Dave turned onto his side, propped his bad knee on an extra pillow and balled another one up under his head. The image of one pretty blonde wouldn't go away, so he fixated on it, on her sky-blue eyes and hot body. He imagined those legs that wouldn't quit, wrapped around his waist, killer heels and all. He could almost feel them digging into his naked butt.

He fisted his cock, tried to fantasize that a hot groupie was blowing him. Instead he saw Diane, her shoulder-length blonde hair tickling his belly as she lowered her face, took his swollen flesh between her soft, wet lips.

Her hair felt like silk beneath his fingers when he cupped her head, encouraged her to take him deep. The warmth of her breath sent shivers through him, made him want much more.

Not just sex but the sensation of them touching shoulder to hip, of her raking her nails down his back then caressing where she'd scratched, as though she wanted more than an orgasm. A relationship. Commitment.

Fuck, he was insane. No good woman, let alone one as gorgeous as Diane, was going to fall for Dave Delaney and take on all his baggage. Trying to put her image out of his mind, Dave tightened his fingers on his cock, beat out a cadence, first slow then faster and harder, until finally he found, if not contentment, then temporary release.

But when he finally slept, he dreamed about Diane.

* * * * *

And he dreamed again the following nights although he'd sworn he wouldn't. It wasn't as though he could avoid seeing Diane. Hedgecock wasn't a big enough place so anybody could be invisible. At the only grocery store on Monday, he had spotted her talking with Melanie Tate in the small produce section. Today when he saw her go into the feed store, he moved as fast as he could to join her, wondering as he crossed the street what he could buy since the store didn't sell dog food and he had no other animals at his place.

He didn't have to torture his brain because she was coming out with a huge sack of something by the time he caught up with her. "Damn, I wish I could help you with that," he said, shooting her his best grin.

"You can. Open up the tailgate on my truck so I can stuff this inside." She indicated a beat-up blue pickup that happened to be parked right at Dave's feet.

The latch thankfully was loose enough that it popped open when he applied one hand, since he dared not set aside both crutches at the same time. "Here you go." When she set the sack down, he helped her push it inside then slammed the tailgate closed.

"Thanks. Usually I try to corral Dylan so he can do the heavy lifting, but today he's still at school."

"I'm just sorry you couldn't have corralled me. I promise, I'm gonna be off these crutches before long, and then I'll be your pack mule."

"Sounds as though you're angling for a part-time job. I'd love to have you but I doubt you'd appreciate the pay."

Dave grinned. "You never know. Maybe I'd want my pay in hugs and kisses and a little bit more."

Diane's cheeks turned a pretty pink. "If you're anything like I remember, you'd be wanting a whole lot more."

"Guilty as charged. I remember kissing you once. You tasted mighty sweet then. I'm anxious to find out if you taste as sweet as I remember."

"A lot of years have gone by." She paused, then met his gaze. "I remember that kiss, too."

"Good. By the way, who's Dylan?"

"He's my son."

During his teenage years, Dave had helped Grandma around the ranch, none too willingly. But he'd done it. Now he tried to imagine DJ helping with chores, but he couldn't. "I hate to say it. My boy's so spoiled he has no concept of honest labor. You're lucky that Dylan helps out."

"I know. He's fourteen going on thirty. Not at all like I remember the boys we went to school with. He'd rather stick his nose in a book than do most anything except take care of the animals. Or watch pro football on TV." A shadow crossed Diane's face. "Sometimes I think maybe he's trying too hard not to be like Frank."

Dave didn't know how to respond to that, so he just shook his head and smiled. "DJ—he's my son—is thirteen. I hope he doesn't pick all my bad traits to imitate."

As they talked he walked Diane to the driver's side of her awful excuse for a truck and opened the door for her to climb in. "Does this thing run?"

She shrugged. "It did until I parked it here. Let's not give it any ideas about making a visit to Artie's Car Repair. Aren't you supposed to be over at school, doing whatever it is that football coaches do?"

"Not until school lets out. Until then I'm all yours if you need me."

When Diane wrinkled her nose at him, she looked cute. And sexy — but nice, too. "I'll have Dylan unload it when he gets home from school. This smelly stuff, as you call it, is fertilizer for my veggie garden. The soil out here's not too kind, so it needs a lot of help."

"Hmmm. Maybe I'll sneak over and steal a tomato or two."

"Feel free, only there won't be any for a couple of months yet. You know, I haven't said it before, but I'm glad you came home."

"Me, too. I'd like to take you out sometime soon, talk about old times. Share some meals, make a few new memories." *And find out if this attraction I'm feeling goes both ways.* "How about it?"

"I'd like that, anytime I can park my son somewhere so he doesn't get ideas that maybe his mom's wanting another man in her life. Come by, or give me a call sometime. You'd better run along now or you'll be late for the first day of spring practice." The smile she shot his way had to have packed at least a thousand watts. As he limped to his silver Escalade, he waved back and grinned. His cock swelled against his jeans.

"Down, boy. This one's a keeper. And she's been burned. Slow and easy — she's no groupie and no one-night stand," he muttered as he slid behind the wheel and started the engine.

Chapter Two

ഔ

Football had been Dave's whole life since he was the age of these boys who'd come out for spring tryouts. Palming a ball, enjoying the familiar feel of the textured leather, he stood by his old coach who'd retired but apparently couldn't stay away from the sport any more than Dave could. "What do you think, Coach? You spot anybody special this afternoon?"

Coach Williams stared at the boys on the field for a long time. "Don't think so, not this year. Of course it would help if you could talk Dylan Granger into playing. Kid's got an arm on him. Big, too, though he's just fourteen."

"Why isn't he out here at tryouts?" As best Dave could recall, every boy at Hedgecock High had gone out for football when he was a kid. Except for one poor kid who'd gotten crippled in an accident at his family's ranch. "I imagine that if Frank were alive, he'd be out here, pushing his boy to play."

Coach shook his head. "Frank was out of the picture at least two years before he died. Diane threw him out. The boy's a real good student, more interested in his studies than football. Shame, though. I imagine he could be good. His dad was a decent lineman back in the day. Too bad he couldn't harness whatever anger it was that drove him."

"Yeah." As Dave recalled, Frank Granger had played dirty—even dirtier than the Maulers lineman who'd recently torn up his knee. "There are too many of them around, for sure. At least you had the balls to throw him off the team my sophomore year."

"Couldn't let the guy cripple somebody. He was a loose cannon, always trying to knock a chip off somebody else's shoulder. But Dylan isn't like that. You ought to talk to him about playing. If nothing else, the kid needs exercise."

Dave had trouble imagining Diane having a son old enough for high school before realizing she could easily have one way older than that. After all, she was only a year or so younger than he was. "Yeah. I could go talk to his mom. There's no doubt the boy has some talent, with Keith being his uncle." That would give Dave an excuse to talk with Diane, see if he could hurry along developing the chemistry he'd sensed sizzling between them.

The old coach's gaze settled on a rut in the playing field. "You need to keep telling the boys to watch out for those ruts. There's a shortage of boys in school this year. You don't need any of them breaking bones on that beat-up field."

"I will. It's got to be damn hard, growing grass around here. Maybe we should try to get the school board to spring for Field Turf." It worked well in outdoor stadiums, so he figured it should do as well on the arid field. "Boys, be careful not to step in those holes," he yelled. With any kind of luck, the school district would raise enough money from the reunion and football camp to update the field as well as the bleachers and field house that hadn't been worked on significantly since he could remember.

Though he'd enjoyed the hell out of the afternoon with the boys, he couldn't deny he was now eager to turn his mind to the pretty blonde who kept invading his dreams.

* * * * *

The Connors place, like everything else Dave had seen since coming home, was just as he remembered it, only a little shabbier. Paint was peeling off the wood trim of the stone-faced ranch house. Times must have been hard for Diane, he decided, glancing at the barn that obviously needed a paint job. Ruts on the drive made him slow to a crawl. Only a couple of horses grazed in the fenced field behind the buildings, but at least they looked healthy and well-fed.

What a nasty-looking bull! The ugly creature stomped and bellowed in a separate paddock away from the horse pasture. Dave made sure he drove past that animal before stopping his SUV and climbing out.

He walked carefully, mindful of what tripping on the uneven ground could do to his bad knee. Though he hated feeling like a timid old woman he held onto the stair rail when he climbed the four steps to the porch. The door swung open before he had time to knock, and Diane greeted him with a smile. "You're a little early for tomatoes, my friend. Seriously, come on inside and tell me what brings you out here so soon?"

"Just chasing down another player for my football team. Unless you object to having your son play." Grateful to get off his feet, Dave sank onto an overstuffed chair and propped his leg on the matching ottoman. Glancing around the living room, he saw more signs of genteel poverty—a worn sofa and arm chair, sagging drapes and a faded blue carpet with a hole half-hidden under the leg of the sofa.

Diane sat on the end of the sofa, her expression challenging. "Stop it. I know you're thinking the place is a wreck. It is. But it's not my brother's fault. He's offered to fix things up. He actually begged me to let him do it when he was here for his wedding. So did our mother, who hates nowhere on Earth as much as she hates this ranch. But it's mine. Daddy left it to me because he knew Mom didn't want it and Keith was just a kid. It's nobody else's fault that I let Frank start a rodeo stock farm here, or that the operation went belly-up not long after he did. And I can't blame anybody because the one oil well on the property went dry a few years back. Dylan and I are getting along just fine. We don't need anybody's charity."

"Actually I wondered. But I remember you always had more pride than sense. I assume that creature you've got penned up outside is a leftover from the stock farm, since I didn't see any cows for him to service." Dave visualized the bull, shuddered when he thought of her having to deal with him.

"Bullyboy? Yes, he is, but he's so gentle nobody would take him when I sold off the rest of the rodeo stock so I guess he's our pet until he dies of old age."

"He sure as hell doesn't look gentle to me. Do you put him out at stud?"

Diane laughed. "He's hardly a purebred, prime specimen. He was bred to fight, but he must have gotten all the peaceful genes from both of his very nasty parents. Besides, since he was born the same day as Dylan, I don't have the heart to sell him for dog food. He's just another member of our family." She paused for a minute. "Could I get you a sandwich and something to drink?"

"Can't say I'd mind. I'm getting tired of cooking for one, but I hate eating out all the time, so I manage."

"You and that frou-frou poodle?"

He grinned as he got up and followed her into the kitchen. "Yeah, it's just me and my little girl's dog. My ex tossed us out together, said we were too much trouble for her to put up with anymore. Daisy doesn't eat nearly as much as Bullyboy, I don't imagine."

"Probably not." When she smiled, it warmed him all over.

He wanted to hear her laugh out loud. "It probably costs me more to keep Daisy groomed than it does for you to feed Bullyboy. I have to drive her all the way to Pecos whenever she needs a trim."

"Poor baby. You, not the dog." She chuckled and struck a comically grave face, though her lips quivered against more laughter. "Did you ever think about grooming her yourself, tough guy? You could even paint her toenails that pretty hot pink."

He liked hearing her laugh. A lot. And it did other things to him as well. If it weren't for his bum knee, he'd chase her around the counter for her teasing, threatening to retaliate. Then he'd kiss her until neither of them could stand.

Instead he answered her as though she were serious. "Yeah, I've thought about doing it myself. I even bought a set of dog clippers a while ago. But Cathy likes to keep her dolled up with the pompoms and such. I doubt I could manage a fancy trim, so..." He shrugged. "There's not a whole lot I won't do to keep my little girl happy. And she expects to see Daisy with all her frou-frou every time we talk on the webcam."

Diane paused, apparently trying to digest the fact that he doted on his daughter. "I hear you've turned your grandma's place into a showplace. Seems a lot of doing unless you're planning to make this your permanent home. Keith said something about you being offered a job doing color commentary for one of the networks."

"I was also offered a gig advertising Viagra, but I told my agent to say thanks but no thanks. I want to stay close to football. Coaching's my best option now, with my knee torn up the way it is. If I get the right offer sometime from a pro team, I may take it, but that's not likely. As Buddy—he's my agent—says, I was too much of a hell-raiser for too long for a team to hire me to coach their innocent babies except out of sheer desperation. I pretty much imagine I'm back in Hedgecock for good."

Diane took a ham and some cheese out of the refrigerator and sliced some onto a plate. "So the swimming pool, fancy gourmet kitchen and gussied-up bedrooms I've heard so much about are just for you?"

"And my kids, when I get them for a couple of weeks each summer. They're not used to roughing it. Rosa, their mom, has always liked living the good life. So have I," he added, not willing to lay all the blame on his ex-wife.

"I see. You want mayo and mustard?"

"Sure." He watched her assemble three sandwiches between thick slices of what looked like homemade bread. "That looks real good. Thanks." What really looked good to Dave was Diane, the perfect, sexy homemaker, a role Rosa rarely had played between concert tours. If Dylan weren't right outside... But he was. Dave doubted Diane would appreciate him scooping her up in his arms while she was setting out food.

"You're welcome. Why don't we sit in here and eat? Dylan should be in from feeding Bullyboy and the horses. You can ask him then if he'd like to go out for the team. He's never played any organized sports. Frank was always away, out on the rodeo circuit, even before we divorced, and I've always considered football a spectator sport."

Dave thought of his boy and DJ's apathy toward the sport that had always kept him in electronic games, golf lessons and the other activities Rosa thought were important. "Most women think that way. Good thing. I doubt too many guys would feel right, knocking the crap out of a girl. If Dylan wants to play, I can spend some time bringing him up to speed with the rules and such. Frankly, I can't imagine any kid with relatives like Keith and Frank wouldn't have a lot of raw talent."

"Yeah. Well... To tell the truth, I've always worried that Dylan might be a bully like his dad. That probably doesn't make a lot of sense..."

"In a way, it does. I'm sure you've got some misgivings. But playing high school ball doesn't necessarily mean a kid's going to end up a pro...or a bully for that matter." Dave reached out, took Diane's hand. The softness of her wrist and the tops of her fingers amazed him since he had a good idea about how hard she must work.

"'Bully' fit Frank right well. And Dylan knows it." When she met his gaze, he saw disappointment and maybe a little guilt. "He doesn't know my brother well enough to form an idea..."

"Keith's no bully. As far as pro football players go, he's one of the cleanest. On top of playing clean, he's never chased groupies or partied hard like a lot of us do. If Dylan needs an idol, he'd do well to pick his uncle."

"Not you if you're his coach? You had a pretty good career, too."

"Yeah. I did. But I was nobody's poster boy for the good guys. Your brother is. Besides, he's still got some years left to play. I'm finished."

Diane frowned. "Keith's team played dirty in the Super Bowl. I saw you get hit. I hope that guy McRae got punished."

Her concern gave Dave a warm feeling. "He got fined, five figures. So did several other defensive players for the Maulers. I can't say I didn't enjoy hearing about the hits to their wallets while I was laid up in the hospital."

"I guess fines like that don't bother you guys a lot, considering how much you earn. I think the League should have suspended them." She stood, as though she needed to put a little distance between them.

"I imagine thirty grand stung McRae pretty good, though it probably won't pauper him. He's not a star—probably plays for veteran minimum. Not all players make the kind of money teams pay their starting quarterbacks. Not that most of us would shrug off a big fine even if we wouldn't feel it as hard as some other players."

"Have you ever been fined?"

Dave shot her a self-conscious grin. "A few times but not for anything I did on the field. I tended to do my hell-raising in other places, especially when I was still young and foolish." He pondered explaining some of the exploits that had cost him money and the respect of some of his coaches but was saved when Dylan came in the back door.

"Hi, Mom. Mr. Delaney. Sorry it took so long to feed the animals. Bullyboy wanted a little extra attention."

Diane indicated the sandwich at the empty place on the table. "Sit down and eat. Dave wants to talk to you about going out for the football team."

"You want me to?" A surprised look crossed the boy's face when he looked over at his mom.

"It's up to you. Dave says he can spend some extra time with you, teaching you the rules and so on. I explained that you've never played before." The way Diane looked at her son, Dave had no doubt that he was pretty much her world. "Of course you'll have to keep up with your studies."

"No problem, Mom. School's easy. I'm just wondering if I'll have time to do my chores and play football, too."

Dave cleared his throat. "I managed to. So did your Uncle Keith, I imagine. Practice is an hour and a half after school every day but Fridays when we have games. If you need a ride home, I can drop you off since my place is right down the road from here." He hoped Dylan would decide to play, not only because the boy would improve the team but also because it would provide more opportunities for Dave to see Diane.

"I'll try out for the team. Mom's telling the truth. I've never played football. I've watched a lot of games on TV, though."

Undoubtedly the kid had seen the Super Bowl where he'd gone down since Keith had been playing for the other team. "High school ball's a little different. I think you'll have fun."

"I'm sure I will. Thanks for offering to help me. I've got to finish polishing up the report that goes with my project for the science fair. See you tomorrow, Mr. Delaney." With that Dylan wolfed down the rest of his sandwich and practically ran out the kitchen door.

Diane shook her head. "He's like that, always in a hurry to get his chores done so he can hit the books."

If only I'd been so interested in my studies, I might have earned a degree in something more marketable than recreation. "You must be very proud of him."

"Yes. Frank wasn't, though. He wanted Dylan to act as macho as he liked to think he was." Diane smiled but Dave saw pain in her blue gaze. "Thanks for coming out and encouraging him to play. Boys need some exercise other than doing chores for their moms."

"No thanks needed. I need him on the team. Not to mention, I wanted to see you again. Is Dylan going on that science-class trip to San Antonio this weekend?"

"Uh-huh. No way would he let me keep him from going to show off his stuff at the district science fair." The sadness drained from her eyes, replaced by obvious pride. "He built a model irrigation system, pipes and water and all. His teacher says it has a good chance of getting a prize at the state science fair next month."

"That sounds like quite a project. I know I said it before, but you must be very proud." Dave paused but held her gaze. "I thought maybe we could go out while Dylan's away. I'll help you do his chores." Dave worried that his knee wouldn't be up to doing a lot, but at least he could make the effort. "At least I'll help with whatever I can do, considering this leg's not quite healed."

"I'd like that." Diane stood, following Dave as he made his way through the living room. "You know, you don't have to go."

He wished he could stay, but he wanted to sample her soft lips, run his fingers through the pale blonde hair that swung just past her shoulders…and more. Much more that wouldn't go over, not with her son likely to walk in on them any minute. "Yeah. I do. How about if I pick you up after practice on Friday?"

"Okay." She stepped up to him, stood on tiptoe and brushed her lips across his cheek. "Much as I love Dylan, I'm looking forward to a break from being Mom. Especially now, since I'll be spending part of that time with you."

"Until Friday then." Dave wanted to kiss her, really kiss her. But he settled for turning his head, briefly joining their lips. Only Diane didn't cooperate. When she held his face and deepened the contact, the little taste he'd expected turned quickly into a deep, tongue-thrusting feast that fired a hunger he had a feeling wouldn't be easy for either of them to deal with until Friday rolled around.

* * * * *

His kiss lasted in her mind long after he'd left her standing on the porch watching his shiny new Escalade bounce down her rutted driveway in a cloud of dust from the worn-down sandstone gravel.

As kisses went, Dave's had started out pretty mild, almost brotherly. But by the time it ended they were both breathing hard and wanting more. Diane's lips still tingled hours later, as though he'd recharged her sleepy libido. She lay in bed, unable to help imagining how Dave's big, calloused hands would feel as they learned all the spots that made her shudder with long-suppressed need.

Strong. Everything about him showed her strength. Not quite perfection but reassuring maleness that fostered desire, not fear. His long fingers bore healed dings and one surgical scar that ran the length of his left index finger and snaked its way to his wrist. Battle wounds, she guessed, like the one that still had him depending on forearm crutches as his knee healed.

He'd told her he had surgery the day after the Super Bowl. Now, around six weeks later, he was still feeling the pain. Damn it, she hated the violence men seemed to relish so much. *Idiot. It isn't like Dave is asking you to marry him. You're only going out on a date. Besides, he's retired now. Even if he weren't, playing football's not likely to kill him. After all, he'd be tangling with other men, not bulls bred to be killers.* Diane curled up under the covers, reminded herself she'd lost Frank—or rather thrown him out—long before she got the call saying he was dead. But she had a feeling it would have hurt a lot more if Frank's untimely demise had followed a happy marriage, not years of misery punctuated with pain and fear for Dylan and herself.

No matter. That part of her life was history she didn't intend to repeat. She touched her cheek, recalled the feeling of Dave's shadow of dark beard stubble against her skin, imagined how it would feel when he suckled her breasts…buried his face between her legs to taste her honey.

Edie used to brag that Dave was an imaginative lover, not afraid to do anything that would make her come. Back then Diane had hidden her jealousy behind childish lies that Frank was equally exciting when they had sex. Now, though…

Now she could hardly wait. The courtship dance would be short, because they were no longer kids. In Dave's kiss she felt banked urgency, much like what she'd experienced at the mere sight of him a week ago at her brother's wedding. No, she wanted to have sex with Dave Delaney and she wouldn't hesitate to let him know it.

She shifted in the bed, her senses heightened. Her old, soft sleep shirt tangled between her legs, brushing flesh that hadn't been touched in lust for far too long. Worn bed linens bound her, limited her motion, let her fantasies take her, carry her away from the daily drudge of keeping this place going and the responsibility for bringing up her son alone.

In her mind the covers were Dave's arms, binding her to his hard body. They were his strong hands, molding her to his heat and strength, his long, muscular legs tangling with hers. The dark dusting of hair on his chest, his thighs, his belly would tickle her, a reminder that this was a man, a capable lover taking her into a world where nothing existed but him— his heat, his strength, his uncompromising maleness conquering her and taking her to a world of hot sensation. Passion.

Yet something more. Diane sensed he wouldn't be satisfied to claim her body. He'd want her soul. That scared her. She wasn't ready to relinquish her hard-earned independence. Probably would never be.

Fool! Wishful thinking, pure and simple. From all she'd heard, Dave might steal hers, but he wasn't a man to offer his soul. It bothered her a lot to know he'd cheated on his wife. Never mind that she'd reportedly cheated on him, too, in some strange celebrity-type arrangement where fidelity apparently wasn't desired or expected.

Momentary pain gave way to relief, and Diane untangled herself from the covers. She sat up, staring out the window at a bright new moon. Dave was the ideal casual lover, easy to desire yet not a likely candidate for permanency.

Exactly what she wanted. A man she imagined must have honed his bedroom skills with the best of them, whose killer smile and hard body could melt the reserve of a nun. A man who'd fulfill all her late-night yearnings for a little while and leave her with memories she'd cherish the rest of her life.

Chapter Three

ꝏ

Where the hell did an adult male take a date in Hedgecock, Texas? Dave lay back in his whirlpool tub, his bad knee positioned to get maximum benefit from the swirling water. Closing his eyes, he imagined taking Diane to the spots he'd visited as a kid, reacquainted himself with in the short time he'd been back here.

He visualized the Burger Den, still the same when he'd eaten there last Monday as it had been years ago—a kids' hangout where the fare consisted mostly of greasy fries, fried chicken and burgers floating in fat. Even the advertising posters on the wall were the same faded ads he recalled from his high school days. Not exactly where he'd choose to feed a woman he wanted to impress.

There was always the café—no name that he'd ever heard of, just "the café". The steaks there came pan-fried and the beer was served in pitchers kept cold with zip-lock plastic bags full of ice. Since coming back, he'd passed a couple of evenings there listening to music from a jukebox and watching a few folks dance on the postage-stamp-size wooden floor. He imagined Diane had, too. It was Hedgecock's version of a family-style gathering place. Not that the café was bad—it was just that Dave didn't particularly want to watch his date dancing with other guys. Too bad his knee wasn't well enough to try a two-step, let alone the spirited line dances he'd watched while nursing a beer at the bar.

There was always the Hedgecock Inn, a small, square sandstone hotel that rose three stories high out near the county line, situated at the intersection of two sleepy blacktop roads. The hotel had been there for nearly a hundred years, when somebody apparently thought Hedgecock was going to grow into a major town. Dave had even been there on prom night and remembered that dinner had cost an arm and a leg, considering his limited teenage budget. He doubted he'd consider the hotel's food that good now or the price high enough to raise concern. As he remembered, the décor had been pretty run-down back then. He imagined it would be shabbier now.

Dave sank as deep as he could into the swirling water, let strong hot streams of water help work kinks out of his shoulders and back following an afternoon of tossing footballs to next year's would-be receivers. Until he could teach Dylan and a couple of the other boys who showed a little potential as quarterbacks how to throw decent spirals, he'd be doing most of the passing—making almost as many throws every day as he'd been doing in pro practice the past couple of years.

Eyes closed, he pictured Diane the way she'd looked that afternoon when she came to pick up Dylan from practice. Was it his imagination or had she changed out of the worn jeans and work shirt she usually wore, to remind him she wasn't always a tomboy? Fuck, he hadn't needed reminding. But he'd liked watching how that pale-blue dress swung against her gorgeous bare legs almost like an invitation. And his fingers had itched to bury themselves in her blonde hair that she'd let loose to brush her shoulders.

He wanted to show her something special tomorrow night. Hell, he wanted them to have a night together that neither of them would be likely to forget. But he didn't want to spend hours driving to San Antonio or Midland, or even to nearby Pecos where he doubted the choice of dining facilities would be much more impressive than the ones right here. Damn, he should have learned to fly and bought himself a plane, like most rich guys who lived in the middle of Texas nowhere.

He could always arrange for a charter over at Billy Joe's crop-dusting and charter service on the other side of town. But then Dave had never been all that keen on flying, particularly in anything smaller than a 737, the model most teams he'd played for usually chartered for cross-country road trips. Besides, he was pretty sure Diane wouldn't be the least bit awed if he flaunted his money. A stubborn expression had taken over her face when she insisted that she wouldn't take any financial help from her brother Keith to fix up her ranch. It was certain she wouldn't take any help from him, either. He doubted she'd even agree to something as insignificant as letting him pay a high school kid to feed and water her horses and that snorting pet bull for the weekend. Which pretty much shot down the possibility of them flying off somewhere romantic for a date.

Hell, he'd just fix dinner here. After all, he liked to cook, which was why he'd included a gourmet kitchen when he decided to renovate. Yeah. Dave imagined sitting on one of the padded loveseats in the garden room next to the kitchen, telling Diane all about the collection of exotic plants Grandma had left in his care. The moon would be glowing overhead and with any kind of luck something would be blooming and it would make the air in the room smell sweet. Maybe they'd even take a swim, although the heater wasn't hooked up yet and he imagined that water would still be too cold for comfort. Daisy would chase fireflies until they bored her. Then she'd make friends with Diane before stretching out on the rug and taking a nap.

He liked the setting he'd just imagined. And he was pretty sure Diane would like it, too. There'd be plenty of time later for San Antonio and Dallas and faraway places he'd love to share with her. Time when they could include Dylan and maybe his own kids in their plans. If he got lucky, he'd even find the time to make up to her for things they hadn't done together when they were young. Visions of lounging lazily at luxurious Baja California resorts, taking in the sights of Paris and Rome... Yeah, he and Diane could do plenty together, all in good time.

His date plan settled, Dave got out of the whirlpool tub, emptied it and toweled dry. First thing in the morning, he'd take some steaks out of the freezer to thaw in the refrigerator, and he'd make sure he had all the stuff he'd need to complete the meal. He'd also change the sheets on his bed. Just in case.

Just in case she was longing for him the way he longed for her. He'd figure a way to give her pleasure without frightening her—just in case he was right and Frank the Bastard hadn't treated her any better in bed than he had anywhere else. For the first time he was almost glad his knee put limitations on how he could move around because he wanted her to feel in control. If she had the least bit of fear, she wouldn't need him pinning her to the bed, making her feel helpless beneath his substantial weight. Nope.

If they made love tomorrow, it was gonna be her way. Meantime he'd work out then rest his knee. Just because he was retired and gimpy didn't mean he intended to let himself go to flab, especially when he had such a good reason to stay in shape.

* * * * *

Diane woke the next morning looking so forward to being with Dave that she barely worried about Dylan being away for four whole days showing off his project at the area science fair. She'd go to the state fair, of course, assuming Dylan made it that far. But she completely trusted the teachers and other parents who'd be watching her son. What was worrying her at the moment was the question of what she was going to wear for her first date since high school.

Not that she had a lot of choice other than the jeans and shirts she wore around the ranch and two dresses she had for PTA meetings and going to the café for the occasional meal out with Dylan. Dave had seen and commented on one of them already earlier this week when she'd decided to dress up a bit to pick up Dylan from football practice. The other one, also blue but a little dressier, she'd worn for Keith and Tina's wedding, so he'd seen it, too.

Of course she could splurge and buy the skirt and top she'd been looking at for months over at Mabel Whatley's general store. By now Mabel would probably be willing to mark it down since she'd most likely have decided it would never fit her or her pretty but plus-sized daughter.

Yes. A date for the first time in more than twenty years was an occasion that called for at least a tiny indulgence. She could make meals from her freezer and pantry shelves for a couple of weeks without starving Dylan or herself. She just hoped Dave didn't show up wearing a suit, planning to take her somewhere far away from Hedgecock for a fancy meal.

Cal Tate had done that when he was dating Melanie last fall. They still took off for a few days in San Antonio or Santa Fe, every month or so. Diane considered how her brother, who lived the same sort of life Dave had recently come home from, thought nothing of packing up Tina and Jack and flying off to some faraway resort on a minute's notice.

"Mom?"

Dylan drew Diane out of her fretting. "What, son?"

"When I fed Bullyboy this morning, I noticed that cut on his leg looks like it's getting infected. You probably need to call the vet."

Oh, damn it anyhow. She'd really wanted that new outfit. But she couldn't let the dumb animal's leg rot off. Though Bullyboy had gashed it on the fence when he decided to scare the daylights out of a property appraiser who'd come too close to his pen two weeks earlier, she owed him proper medical care. "All right. Do you have everything you need?"

"Yeah. You already sent in the money for the trip. And I saved a few dollars of this week's lunch money just in case. I'll be fine. Gotta go. I hear the bus coming around the corner." One fast hug and Dylan was on his way.

"Be good."

Dylan grinned. "I will. See you Monday."

* * * * *

"Okay, boys. Pack it in for today and enjoy the weekend." With nearly a third of his team off on the science trip, there didn't seem to be a lot of reason to keep the remaining boys around until five. Dave figured he could head out to Diane's place and help her with whatever needed doing before they could start their night out.

A few minutes later he pulled in behind a dusty van parked next to Bullyboy's pen and made a wide circle around the far side of it. No way did he want to encounter the bull any sooner than he had to. "Diane?" he called out.

Then he saw her. She was holding the ring through the animal's nose and talking quietly to him while a gray-haired man did something to his broad, forbidding-looking shoulder and front leg.

"Hi, Dave. You're early. Hold on, Doc Evans is about finished here. I'll meet you up on the porch." She sounded a little distressed, as though he was too early and she wasn't ready.

He couldn't help feeling relief that he wasn't the one within reach of the huge animal's sharp horns and wicked hooves, but it scared him half to death to see Diane so close to the bull. She seemed to know what she was doing, though. Impressed by her competence and gentleness, and watching her pet Bullyboy's head, Dave couldn't help thinking about how well she'd soothe another big male animal with those fingers — or work him up.

He made his way to the porch and waited while Diane paid the vet and sent him on his way. "Is Bullyboy sick?" he asked when she joined him, pretty even with dirt on her face and her boots caked with mud.

"He cut his leg a couple of weeks ago. Unfortunately it got infected so he had to get an antibiotic injection. He didn't much like Doc Evans going into his pen, so…" She shrugged, looked down at the dirt she'd accumulated and shook her head. "I need to go shower before I'm fit to be around."

"What needs doing?"

She smiled up at Dave. "Nothing, unless you'd like to help clean me up. I went ahead and took care of the horses before Doc arrived, and Bullyboy has plenty of food in his trough." Her cheeks turned fiery red when she apparently realized what she'd just said.

Dave moved closer, trapping her between the rail and his body. "Is that an invitation?" he asked, his imagination working overtime, picturing him and her together in a steaming shower, him rubbing his soapy hands all over her lush body. Just the idea of it had him getting hard. "I wouldn't mind if it was."

She wedged first one boot then the other between two porch rails. "You'd be sorry. I'm a mess. I'd hoped to be finished and cleaned up before you got here."

He eased back, giving her space when he saw she was getting flustered. "I couldn't wait. I thought you'd let me help with the chores." He bent, gave her a quick kiss. "You're one damn exciting woman, mud or no. Go ahead, take your shower if you're sure you don't want my help. If it's okay with you, we'll eat at my place. If not, I guess it will have to be the Hedgecock Inn."

"I don't mind. I've heard about all the remodeling you had done and I've been dying to get a look. To tell the truth, I wouldn't mind taking a swim in that pool I've heard so much about. Come on in the front room and watch TV while I clean up. I won't take long."

Dave imagined them playing naked in the pool but thought better of the idea since the water temperature was hovering around sixty-five degrees, like the early March air. The hot tub in his master bathroom was almost big enough to swim in, if a swim was what his lady wanted. Oh yeah, that would work just fine if he could only be patient and wait, instead of plotting seduction like a horny teenager.

He tried to cool off his libido by watching the local news from Pecos. Not that there was much for the newscaster to talk about—a bar fight that sounded tamer than an average NFL game except for some of the participants winding up in jail and advance promo for an upcoming amateur rodeo featuring kids from area high schools. When he heard Diane coming downstairs he stood and held out both hands.

A vision in jeans and a pink top that draped over her shoulders and breasts, she came into his arms, no hesitation, as though she were as anxious as he to get on with getting better acquainted. "You clean up real good," he said, taking in her light, sweet scent and the softness of cheeks rosy more from excitement than from something out of expensive little jars like the ones that used to litter his ex-wife's makeup table. "Ready?"

"Do I need to bring anything?"

"Just yourself." He'd have suggested a change of clothes but figured she'd look just as good wearing one of his T-shirts, or nothing at all. "I've got steaks ready to cook. Mel Tate helped me snatch one of the peach pies they sell in the cafeteria at school for our dessert. They taste as good now as they did when we were kids. In case you don't want me nibbling on you for dessert."

She stood on tiptoe, nibbled at his earlobe. "How about me nibbling on you? I always used to wonder if you'd taste as good as you looked."

Her enthusiasm surprised him but he liked it. A lot. "Be my guest, anytime. We'd better go before I decide we don't need to eat and get it on with you right here. God but you're one dynamite lady." Part of him again wished he'd acted on the attraction he'd felt toward her when they were kids, but mostly he was glad to be getting a chance now that they were all grown up and unattached.

She pulled away when he tightened his hold a little and shot him a serious look. "Let's go to your place. I don't want old memories to taint the pleasure I know I'll have with you."

* * * * *

The pleasure I know I'll have with you. Diane's words echoed in Dave's head while he drove to his place and parked in the garage. Before she could open her door, he made an admonishing noise and, despite his crutches, came around the outside and opened her door. He was going to treat her right. No excuses. He could tell she appreciated the gesture, too, by the way her eyes sparkled and her cheeks pinkened like a girl's. She touched his hand as she hopped down to the concrete floor.

"Like what you've seen so far?" he asked, taking her hand and herding her into the kitchen.

"What's not to like? I love the sandstone slabs on all the outside walls and the way it's built to look a little like some old-style Mexican hacienda. The kitchen's gorgeous and huge. You must enjoy cooking."

"Yeah. Not so much just for me, but I figure when the kids come visit, I'll be spending a bunch of time in here." He set down his crutches, opened the refrigerator and took out the steaks he'd thawed. "Want a quick tour before I start grilling our dinner?"

"Sure. I'd love seeing how the other half lives. All this space...and everything brand-new." She glanced around the kitchen, her gaze settling on the Jenn-Air grill next to where he'd set out the meat on a polished black granite countertop.

While he imagined most women would love the size and grandeur of the place, he remembered Diane wasn't most women. Trying to see the place through her eyes, he saw not so much a comfortable home as a sandstone-slab monument to his success as a pro athlete. "Not quite everything. Most of the original house was in pretty bad shape, but I wanted to keep the front porch and living room the way Grandma had them." Somehow that was important, he hoped as much so to Diane as it had been to him. "Come this way."

When he laid a hand at her waist, she turned and looked up at him as if she were reading his mind again. "I know you're filthy rich but I like you anyhow. Just because I don't choose to live off my brother's charity doesn't mean I begrudge him his success. Or that I resent you for having made a ton of money, either, for that matter."

Dave loved the way she smiled, the warmth she exuded when she cupped her hand over his chin and stood on tiptoe to give him a quick kiss. "I was worried there for a minute," he told her, tightening his hold on her and drawing her against his uninjured left side. "Come on, I'll show you the rest."

"Don't you need your crutches?"

"Not around the house, as long as I'm wearing my knee brace. The crutches are mainly to keep me from losing my balance on unfamiliar ground." He walked her back through the kitchen and garden room and opened another door so she could see the game room and beyond it, a lap pool and sauna inside a courtyard open to the sun and stars. "The heater isn't hooked up yet, but if you want, we can take a swim anyhow."

"I didn't bring a suit." From the way she looked at the sparkling water, he was pretty sure she did want to jump right in.

"That's okay. There's nobody here to see us if we want to skinny-dip."

"I don't know…"

He came up behind her, wrapped both arms around her waist. "I do. Think of it this way, honey. A long time ago, the kids in this town spent a good many hours screwing like minks under the bleachers at the high school field. A lot more folks could have seen us there than can see us skinny-dipping here, inside an eight-foot-high privacy wall."

She laughed when he bent and blew on her slender neck. "Speak for yourself. I never got naked under the bleachers. Not completely, anyhow." Then she went silent and her body suddenly stiffened beneath his hands. "Stop that!"

"Stop what?" He had no clue what he'd just done to piss her off.

"Stop reminding me of times I'd just as soon forget. For me, those teenage games were the prelude for…oh, never mind." As though she were consciously trying to loosen up, she turned in his arms and laid her head on his chest. "Just let's not take a trip down memory lane tonight, okay?"

She didn't have to say Frank's name and he didn't want that to be part of their evening, either. So he spoke from the heart. "Okay by me. What I want is to make some new memories. With you." He tunneled one hand through her hair, turned her head so her soft breath tickled his skin through his open collar. "Please." When she lifted her head he took her mouth, nibbling gently at first then coaxing her to open for his tongue.

She tasted good. He felt her relaxing in his arms, found her eager yet sweet and almost innocent. Her fingers tightened on his neck, shy encouragement that made him deepen the kiss, move her closer until their bodies came together, her soft curves brushing his growing hardness. He had to stop now while he still could because she deserved slow, careful loving, not the desperate fucking his body was starting to demand.

Especially since everything she'd said and he'd heard around town made him pretty damn sure old Frank had made her life miserable in bed as well as everywhere else. That pissed him off, made him wish her ex were still around so he could exact a few pounds of flesh in her name.

He didn't think she'd like for him to express that, so he kept his tone light. "Maybe we'd better wait to try the pool. The water in it comes from an underground spring, and it's damn cold. Daisy jumped in a few days ago and bounced right back out like she'd been shot out of a cannon. Let me settle you down with Grandma's plants and a glass of wine while I shower and change — unless you'd like to join me."

"I think I'll enjoy the garden room while you change. Not that I'm not tempted to check out your shower." She had a gorgeous mouth, especially when she smiled.

"Probably a good choice, or we might miss out on dinner." Dave took a split of Taittinger Prestige from the refrigerator, popped the cork and poured two flutes. "I hope you like sparkling rosé. One of my coaches sent me off with a case of these little bottles. It's champagne, pinker and sweeter than the Brut they served at Keith's wedding."

He picked up both glasses and handed her one. "Enjoy. I'll be back cooking dinner before you have time to miss me. Hope you don't mind me not dressing up for you."

"Of course not. I'd feel silly if you put on a suit while I'm wearing jeans."

"Think a fresh pair of jogging pants, honey. My jeans won't fit over the brace, at least not without a lot of time-consuming gyrations."

"All right. I like to see you looking like what you are — an incredibly hot jock."

She knew how to make him feel good. "Thanks. I'll be right back as soon as I clean up."

"I'll be waiting."

When she took a sip of wine and smiled, Dave knew he'd chosen well. He'd had the feeling Diane wasn't a wine connoisseur, also the feeling that she went for the substance, not the frills.

* * * * *

When Dave came back downstairs and started grilling steaks, Diane came inside. He looked great in a navy blue Rebels jersey and matching loose jogging pants. He had white Reeboks with red and navy blue stripes — ones she thought she recalled having seen him advertising last season. With his black hair glistening and damp, he could have come straight from the shower after a game. "You're quick. You showered before I finished my champagne." She took one last sip and set the flute on the granite counter by the sink.

"I wanted to get back to you. How do you want your steak?"

Diane glanced at the grill. "Warm."

"Good. It's done, then." Dave lifted the two steaks onto a platter and held it out to her. "You can help here, by setting this on the table." He'd set it earlier, she guessed, because once she put the meat on plates, everything was ready. Ready and as good as anything she'd ever eaten.

"You make food that's better than anything at the café." The thick strip steak was tender as could be, grilled to perfection and served with a savory, sweet-hot sauce that had a hint of peppers and some spice Diane couldn't quite identify. Everything seemed to have come from Dave's own kitchen—even a Caesar salad and the big twice-baked potato they shared—except the peach pie from the school cafeteria. Though she didn't often imbibe, the Pinot Noir from Williams Selyem Winery in California that Dave had chosen tasted wonderful and added a glamorous touch to their meal.

"Thanks. I like to cook. Early on in my career, I learned I couldn't live on fast food and stay in shape—and I was married to a woman who didn't have a clue what a kitchen looked like, much less how to use it. Not to mention that Rosa had a cook who only did Mexican food and went along on all her concert tours. Want some more wine?"

When she nodded, he topped off her glass then poured the rest of the bottle into his. "To us," he said, tapping the stemmed glasses together.

Considering she'd been trying to approach this as a temporary fling, Diane wasn't sure she was ready for "us", though she couldn't deny the uneasy feeling that "us" sounded good. She wouldn't worry about getting carried away, though. Dave wasn't likely ready for "us", either. Not beyond the pleasures of the night that promised to come soon, as the sun was dropping quickly in the western sky. She took a sip of the wine, liquid courage to grab for the pleasure he offered now and not worry about tomorrow. "To tonight."

"I'll drink to that, but to tomorrow, too." It seemed Dave was determined to keep her wondering if tonight was the beginning of something more rather than just a quick fix for both of them. He stood, held out a hand. "Let's go out and see if any of Grandma's flowers are smelling good tonight. A lot of the orchids only have fragrance at night."

"You sent her most of these, didn't you?" After they sat on a padded wrought iron loveseat, Diane inhaled the spicy-sweet scent of an orange-and-burgundy hued orchid hanging on a sandstone tree. "She always used to talk about how hard it was to make them bloom again after the first time."

"I guess Rosa picked most of them. More likely she just called a florist in Pecos and had something sent out for every occasion that called for flowers. Rosa likes orchids, the way a lot of women seem to go for roses. Daisy, no!"

When Diane shifted her gaze she found the poodle sitting, looking ashamed of herself as she held onto a spiny leaf she'd separated from a big plant by the door. "Go on, do your thing outside. Grandma would tan your curly hide if she found you messing with her flowers."

Even though Dave sounded stern, Diane doubted he'd let anybody, even his late grandmother, mess with the usually well-behaved poodle. "It's nice to see you love your dog. I kind of worried, after watching you cringe around Bullyboy."

Dave chuckled. "I tried bull riding once at an amateur rodeo years ago. Haven't cared much for the critters since I got bounced off on my butt. Daisy doesn't outweigh me by a thousand pounds, and she doesn't have foot-long horns she could ram right through me. Besides, I'd be good to her even if I didn't love her because my little girl made me promise."

Promises. Obviously Dave kept his, at least to his kids. And he'd made sure his grandma got presents, even if he'd had his former wife pick out most of them. Diane felt his arm slide behind her and laid her head against his knuckles, turned her face so she could taste him.

He seemed in no hurry, willing to go at her pace, to enjoy the closeness, watch a gentle breeze ruffling graceful leaves and feel it lifting their hair, tangling the strands lazily together. Frank would have fucked her by now, oblivious to everything but getting off as fast as he could. "I think you're a good man," she said, nipping at Dave's long, lean forefinger and savoring the unique taste of him.

"I want to be, for you." When he spoke, his warm damp breath tickled her earlobe. "Over the years I've had sex with a good many women but I've made love with very few. I've had enough mindless sex to last a lifetime. I want us to make love."

"Now?" Diane blew on his palm, felt his pulse quicken.

He tightened his arm around her, laid his chin on her head. "Whenever you're ready. Tell me, what's got you trembling?"

"Anticipation. Fear…"

"Fear? Baby, I'd never hurt you." Shifting on the loveseat, he looked her in the eye. "What the hell has somebody put in your head about me?"

She lifted her hand to his lips. "It's not you, Dave."

"Then what has you scared of me?"

"I've…I've never enjoyed sex but I so much want to—with you."

He cupped her chin, his warm fingers steadying her. "That bastard—"

"Don't go there. Please." She couldn't stand having him bring up the ghost of her miserable past. "Just help me make some new memories to wipe the old ones away."

He pulled her onto his lap, his grip sure but definitely not threatening. "I'll give it my best shot. Now's the time I'd scoop you up and carry you to my bed to show you how big and strong I am, except my knee's not big and strong at all right now. Let's get Daisy in for the night, and I'll show you where we're gonna play." When he took her mouth and claimed it in a long kiss full of promise, a curl of warmth surrounded her, chased the worst of her fears away. For the first time in longer than she could remember, Diane felt safe. Loved.

Then he set her on her feet and stood. "Here, Daisy. C'mon in, it's bedtime," he said after opening the garden-room door and stepping back when the dog bounded through. "She'll go to her room. Watch."

Daisy trotted up the stairs, pausing at the top. "She moves fast," Diane commented as she and Dave made their way at a slower pace. "Does she sleep with you?"

"Nope. Her bed's in Cathy's room. I haven't been able to coax her to join me even when I let her play in my hot tub. I think she recognizes some of Cathy's things, like the bed and chest I had shipped from Savannah. That's a good girl," he told the dog, bending to scratch her neck then opening the door for her when she barked.

"Woof to you, too," Dave said to the dog. "See you in the morning. Sleep tight."

Through the open door Diane got a glimpse of a room done in pink and lime green, with a big porcelain ballerina on the shelf next to a long, narrow window. Daisy made her way to a fluffy pink dog bed set at the foot of a people bed that was strewn with pillows and stuffed animals. Daisy had her own big rawhide bone on the floor beside her bed.

"Cathy likes girly frills—she hasn't been here yet but she picked out the colors, in case you're wondering. DJ's more into electronic stuff. His room's down the hall, and there's a guest room between them. Come on, here's where I hang out." He opened another door, stepped back to let her go inside.

Chapter Four

 භ

His large bedroom was sparsely furnished, just a king-size bed, a pair of nightstands and a couple of tall-boy chests. Some serious-looking workout equipment occupied the corner opposite the bed, and a huge flat-screen TV hung on the wall nearest to the foot of the bed. She liked the way a soft-looking comforter echoed various colors from the sandstone outer walls—beige and cream with brownish-red and dark gray highlights. Silky-looking dark-brown sheets and pillowcases peeked out from beneath the comforter, reminding her of smooth milk chocolate. *More like temptation*, she thought when Dave folded back the coverlet, sat on the edge of the bed and bent to untie his shoes.

His motions were sure, efficient. No wasted effort or macho posturing. Whether consciously done to put her at ease or simply his usual way, he was doing a good job at calming her nerves. A muted sound of rushing water called her attention to an open door to the side of the chrome gym stuff. "What--"

"That's the hot tub. The jets turn themselves on this time every day." He lifted his injured leg, wincing a little as he pulled off a white athletic sock. Somehow seeing his bare feet, long and narrow, made him seem vulnerable, eased her feeling of susceptibility to his superior strength. "Come here, let's fool around a little. If you want, we can try out the hot tub later."

She kicked off her sandals and sat beside him, surprised at the gentleness in his touch as he laid her across the bed and stretched out beside her. He stroked her over her clothes, his hands sure yet not at all threatening even when he found and caressed the upper curve of her breast. "Mmmm, that feels so good."

"Yeah, you do feel real good. May I?" He slipped a finger under the neckline of her shirt then paused as though waiting for permission.

"Please do." She concentrated on the warm rasp of his fingertips on each inch of skin he exposed. His breathing, shallow and growing rapid, gave her the only hint that what he was doing was arousing him, too. He lay on his side, facing her, his gaze like blue fire as he played with the front fastener of her bra until it gave way and bared her to the waist.

"God but you're even more beautiful than I imagined." He cupped one breast in his big hand, bent and drew the nipple into his mouth. With a degree of care she'd never experienced before, he sucked gently, careful not to graze her tender flesh with his teeth. When Frank had bitten her breasts she'd hated it, but Dave's slow, tender exploration had her growing wet, her tissues swelling.

She wanted to see him, too, to touch the warmth of skin stretched taut over muscles hewn by years of daily exertion. Feeling no fear that the least bit of aggressiveness on her part would turn him into a mindless sex machine, she slid one hand under his T-shirt and splayed her fingers over his ridged belly. "You're one hot man. No wonder all the women—"

"You're the only woman I'm thinking about now. Go on. Touch me. I'm all yours." When he covered her free hand and drew it to his lips, the last of her worries slipped away. "Tell me what you want."

"You." His tight abs rippled beneath her fingers as she ran them over his skin, felt the warmth, the softness of a light dusting of hair. "I like that you don't have a lot of body hair." Somehow she'd assumed that because he was dark-haired, he'd be much furrier. She liked the tickle of the soft hair on her fingertips.

He slipped off his shirt and rolled onto his back, lifting her on top of him. His arms tightened around her like a vise, but she wasn't afraid even though she felt his hard sex pressing into her lower abdomen. Not tentative yet not urgently demanding, either. "I like everything about you. But then you can tell, can't you?" He slid his big hands down, pressed close enough that she could feel him throbbing through their clothes.

"I can tell. You know, you don't have to be quite so careful with me. I won't break."

"I think you might. You said you've never liked sex but that you want to…so it's up to me to see that you enjoy being with me tonight. Are you having fun yet?"

"Oh, yes. But you must be…uncomfortable." He was so hard but he seemed in no hurry.

He laughed then tightened his grip on her hips. "I'll live. Foreplay's a big part of lovemaking, at least for me. Yeah, I want to get inside you. But first I want to taste every inch of your gorgeous body, and I want you to want me so much that you'll beg me to help you come."

His warm breath on her throat when he spoke sent tiny shudders of anticipation all the way to her core. "I think I already do."

"You don't yet. But you will." She loved how he felt, calloused hands and soft skin stretched over rigid muscles. Strong yet tender, she loved the way he held her, coaxing the response that was building, bubbling deep in her core.

The way he ran his hands up over her jeans to the tingling skin of her bare back made her want him to cover her, claim her. Now. There was no meanness, no force, no sense of entitlement to whatever it was he wanted. "I want you now," she murmured, following up the plaintive statement by nibbling at his lower jaw, loving the scratchy feeling of beard stubble on her lips.

"Do you?" He slid a hand down, under the back waistband of her jeans. "I want to taste you here, on your firm, round butt. Your skin's so soft, I'll bet it tastes as good as it feels." Ever so gently he circled her waist, found the snap and zipper and released them, but instead of shoving them down he splayed his fingers over her belly, stroked her as though she were a favorite kitten, incredibly fragile. Extraordinarily cared for.

She wanted him to move lower, and when he did, he tangled his fingers in her pubic hair. "I hope you don't mind that I don't shave down there." Mel had told her how much Cal liked her pussy naked, and she wondered if Dave preferred that, too.

"Your pussy? No, baby, you're so soft there I can hardly wait to go down on you. I don't shave my crotch, either, but I've done it before and wouldn't mind doing it again if you wanted me to. It's a different feeling, not having any hair in the way…but not necessarily better. If you're ready for us to get naked, raise up and shimmy out of those jeans. On second thought, roll off me. Taking off my pants over the knee brace takes some doing and I pretty much have to be sitting up to get it off without causing a bunch of collateral damage."

"Oh." She rolled over and glanced at his bad leg then wriggled out of her jeans and panties. "I hope I didn't hurt you."

"No, honey. I'll live. Not much can mess up the doc's handiwork as long as I've got the brace on. My knee doesn't look pretty, though." He set his dark-blue gaze on her, grinned. "You're the pretty one. Here, help me get these pants off."

"Okay. Tell me if I hurt you." She worked down his elastic-waist jogging pants, gasping when she first saw his long, thick sex jutting forward from a dark nest of curls. Any thought she might have had about getting a good look at his knee flew right out of her brain. His sex was ready even if he pretended to be in no hurry, with a drop of milky fluid glistening in the single eye. And it was beautiful, as beautiful as all the other parts of him.

She'd never thought that about Frank, but then he'd never given her much of a chance to look before he got down to business.

She wanted to taste Dave. She didn't understand why because she'd hated it when Frank forced her to suck his cock. Maybe it was because Dave hadn't even asked her, hadn't pushed her beyond what her own body wanted her to do. She bent her head, tasted him with her tongue. Wanted more.

Curious and more aroused than she could remember ever having been, she bent farther, molded her lips around the purplish head of his penis.

"Omigod, honey." He let out a tortured-sounding moan, and she sensed him working faster to unfasten the heavy metal and leather brace she'd been surprised to learn started just below his right hip and extended to his ankle. "No, don't stop. I'll get this damn thing off—just another minute. The hell with it, I'll leave it on for now."

Moaning, lifting his hips to her mouth, he lay back, his big hands bracketing her face. With passion but without force.

She wouldn't stop. Didn't want to. Emboldened now, she tangled her fingers in his dark pubic curls with one hand while she found his heavy sac and stroked it with the other. There was something about loving him this way, something arousing, something that made her hot and wet as no other man ever had. She wanted Dave inside her, wanted to know he was feeling the pleasure, too.

The pleasure of the sex act, mutually given and taken, with love.

Maybe not the forever kind of love but the kind that transcended the moment, providing a glow she knew wouldn't fade as soon as the act itself was over. Diane slid her mouth down on his cock and swallowed, tentatively at first. But she didn't gag. Relaxing her throat, she took him deep then moved up and down on his turgid length. Loving his strength and his gentleness, reveling in the generous way he'd made her want him…want this.

"Turnaround's fair play," he growled as he sat up and wrestled the brace off his leg, letting out a yelp when he hit his knee with the brace while tossing it to the floor. He lay back again, let her suck him for a few minutes. Then he lifted her backside and growled, "Straddle my face. I'm hungry, too."

When she settled over his face and lowered her sex to his mouth, she felt his heat, the slickness of his tongue when he flailed her clit. "Mmmm. You're wet and hot for me. I love it." Before she could protest, he cupped her ass and drew her down hard on his mouth, finding her pussy and stabbing his tongue inside. Embarrassed yet feeling hotter, needier than she ever had before, she ran her tongue down the length of his shaft then swirled it around the plump, rigid head. More milky, salty lubrication bathed her throat as he dug his fingers into her buttocks and held her when she'd have squirmed to get more of his delicious attention—or to alleviate the timidity she couldn't help feeling when she thought how they must look, feasting as they were on each other's most intimate parts.

Suddenly he pulled back, his big body trembling. "Diane. Stop now unless you want me to come in your mouth." His hot breath made her clit swell and harden, but she didn't obey immediately. When she did, he lifted her off him and swore softly. "Sorry. I can't move a lot with the brace off my knee. Need a condom. There's one in the nightstand drawer." Diane hadn't even thought about protection but she was glad Dave had. She reached over toward the drawer he pointed out and dug around until she found a small plastic-wrapped package that she placed in his hand.

She felt her cheeks burning. Looking at his rigid cock, still glistening wet from her mouth. It had seemed so natural and right a moment ago but a little voice inside her tried to tell her she'd done something wrong, something so pleasurable it must be forbidden—made her suddenly aware of her own nakedness. Of the hot, slick wetness between her legs.

When he ripped open the wrapper and rolled the latex barrier over his erection, he felt her withdrawing emotionally.

"Don't go shy on me now," he said, keeping his tone light. "Come on, climb aboard."

She just looked at him, confusion evident in her expression.

Had the bastard she'd been married to only shown her one way to have sex? Dave didn't doubt that was possible. Frank had never struck Dave as being particularly bright or anxious to please anybody but himself. It made sense that he'd have carried that same attitude that had him kicked off the high school football team over into bed.

"We're gonna do this with you on top, honey. That way we can go as fast or slow as you want." He shot her a self-deprecating grin. "Not to mention my knee and the fact I'm pretty much at your mercy." Reaching over, he caught her at the waist and lifted her over him. "Easy now, come down slow and let me inside."

"I don't want to hurt you." She moved, slow motion, until she collided gently with the tip of his cock. Using one hand, he took hold of his erection and guided the blunt head to the wet heat of her sweet pussy. "Oh, yes."

Good. She liked it. He hadn't been sure she would. "Sink down on me. There's no way you can hurt me unless you suddenly decide to stop. That's it, take me all the way. God you're tight and so hot." When she took him so deep that her outer lips pressed hard on the base of his cock, he steadied her with both hands at her waist, watched her nipples tighten into rigid points that begged for his mouth. "I'm all yours, move however it makes you feel good."

Her moves were tentative, unpracticed, but they were getting him hotter than the most skilled groupie he'd ever fucked. He wanted to lift his hips, slam into her pussy hard and fast, control their lovemaking. But even more, he wanted her to feel at ease, know that with him, making love was a two-way street that she could travel without the stark fear he'd sensed whenever the subject of her ex had come up.

She stilled on him, met his gaze. "Help me, I don't know how…"

"I know, honey. Relax and enjoy the ride. I'll make you feel real, real good." He slid his hands lower and cupped her ass, brushing the tips of his fingers around her damp, warm rim. Taking control, he gripped her butt cheeks, directed her movement up and down on his cock. Slow at first, then faster, harder, he ground their bodies together then lifted her practically off him, only to slam her back down again. Each time he brought her down on him, he pressed one finger against her anal sphincter, going a little deeper each time until he had it embedded to the second knuckle in her rear hole.

Her vaginal muscles tightened on his cock, and when he felt the first spasms of her climax he slid another finger up her ass while moving her on him, thrusting deep, taking her mouth and fucking it with his tongue, feeling rather than hearing her moans of satisfaction. While she still spasmed around his cock, his own climax claimed him, a long series of staccato bursts that left him drained yet more satisfied than he'd been in years. Not wanting to let go of a sense of closeness he hadn't felt for ages, Dave slid his hands up her back, drew her flush against his chest.

"You're a wonderful lover. Thank you." Her soft voice resonated against his shoulder, gave him a sense of pride along with humility that he'd managed to wipe away whatever bad feelings she might have had toward having sex — at least for the moment.

"Thank *you*. Let's rest a few minutes then do it some more." He ran his hands along her spine, loved the silky feel of her skin almost as much as he enjoyed feeling her breasts pressing into his chest, the nipples still so hard he wished he had the energy to move enough so he could suckle them.

"I never realized I might like having my rear end played with. Or that it would feel so good to have you use your mouth on me down there." She raised her upper body, used one hand to explore his chest and nipples. "Your hair's so soft, I like the way it feels on my skin."

His nipples had never been particularly sensitive, and he was glad, because if they were he'd have been hard again in no time. "There are a lot of things we can do when we make love that you may like even better," he said, catching one of her hands and bringing it to his lips. "Some of them will have to wait until my knee gets back closer to normal."

"I can't imagine…"

He could. And he wanted to show her every trick he knew, see the look of wonder on her gorgeous face when he kept her coming for hours on end. "Don't go anywhere, I'll be right back." Hopping along to the bathroom, he disposed of the condom and washed his hands. When he came back to bed, she'd turned on the DVD player. She was watching, wide-eyed, the beginning of a porn film he'd forgotten was in the machine. *Shit.* "I'm sorry, honey."

"Sorry? Why?" She did seem to be interested in the film, in a clinical sort of way.

"Because I forgot to put that video away."

She smiled at him then returned her gaze to the giant-screen TV. "You don't think I should watch it?"

He sucked one of her fingers into his mouth then released it. "It's okay with me if you enjoy watching. Sometimes it's exciting, watching. At the very least you may get some ideas you think you might like for us to try. This one's pretty raunchy. You sure you wanna see it?"

"Uh-huh. I can always use ideas for ways to please you."

He loved her attitude. "Then lie back and take a look. See if you like it. It's okay if you don't — I understand not too many women are into voyeurism, either live or on disk."

When she rolled onto her back next to him and tucked a pillow under her head, he put one arm around her and pulled her close. "Need some covers?" he asked, hoping she didn't because he liked seeing her there beside him, naked and flushed, her blonde hair tangled and her sky-blue eyes bright.

"Not if you don't." When the video started, she reached over and took his hand then let him slide it over to rest on his belly, just above his half-hard cock. "He's...huge," she said when the camera zeroed in on a naked porn star who was completely shaved, head to toe.

Dave laughed. "He's probably not much bigger than I am, it just looks that way because he's shaved off all the hair from around his cock and balls. Do you like the way he looks?"

When she didn't answer right away he figured his own pubes might not be long for the world. But then she gasped when an equally naked woman came in and attacked the man's crotch. Opening her red lips wide, she went not for the cock but for the smooth ball sac, sucking first one testicle then the other in while she lay between his legs and fondled his hard-on with both hands.

"Do you like it when a lover does that?" Diane asked. She sounded halfway between interested and mortified.

Dave did but he'd only had a few women focus their attention on his balls. "It's not something I'd ask a lover to do, but to be honest, the few times a partner did it to me, it felt good. Look, there's another guy joining them." This one was hairless, too, and he had a ring in his well-greased, average-sized cock—and a big cock-shaped strap-on positioned directly behind his balls.

"Oh, my." The second actor bent over the woman and squeezed her large, round tits, saying as he did that he was about to stuff her cunt and ass. "He wouldn't, would he?"

"Yeah, he will. And she'll like it. Not that I imagine there are many women who'd want that. Or many men who'd get off on it, for that matter." Sensing Diane's discomfort at the action on the screen, he drew her close when the woman moaned and reared back, apparently relishing the double penetration.

"Have you ever done that?" Diane's voice registered shock as she watched the woman let go of the first guy's balls and swallow his monster cock.

"Used a strap-on? No. Would you be shocked if I had?"

She sounded nervous when she laughed. "I don't know. I've heard how you used to party…and that you and your wife used to…"

"The word is 'swing'. You're right. We used to like experimenting with different partners. I wasn't averse to sampling some of the groupie pussy I ran into on the road. Rosa didn't mind because she liked variety, too. Most of her lovers were musician types she ran into at work. I've played around with two women at the same time, and once in a while a teammate and I used to double up on one groupie."

"Why did you divorce if neither one of you expected fidelity?" When Diane glanced at the screen where a third man had just arrived and shoved his cock up the first man's ass, she yelped. "Omigod. Has anybody ever done that to you?"

He hesitated because she sounded horrified. He wouldn't lie, though. Not to her. "Once. Because Rosa wanted to get it on with the guy's wife while she watched him fuck me in the ass. That was a long, long time ago." Dave felt his cheeks getting hot. Maybe it hadn't been a good idea to show Diane the porn because she probably was getting the idea that he still wanted to fuck around that way. "I'm shutting this off so we can talk," he said as he made the screen go blank and rolled onto his side so he could concentrate on watching the expressions on her sweet face.

"As for why we split up, Rosa wanted me to quit playing football and go on her concert tours with her. I was determined to keep playing even after I'd done a number on my knee. Not this last time but a few years ago. I guess we grew apart. We probably would have had a better shot at forever if we'd concentrated on pleasing each other and nobody else."

Diane rolled to her side and ran her hand down his leg, stopping at the large raised scar on his knee. "Did you want forever?"

"At one time I thought I did. So did she. We cut out the swinging after a few years and had DJ and Cathy. But I guess we were too used to fucking around, especially when our work kept us apart so much. Our divorce was friendly, as divorces go."

When she moved her hand back up his leg and cupped his balls, his wrung-out cock came back to life. "I don't think I could 'swing'. I'd be embarrassed, watching stuff like what was going on in that video."

He stilled her hand then moved it to a safer spot on his chest. "I d never ask you to. Tell the truth, I decided after the divorce that if I ever tried marriage again, it would be the old-fashioned way—just the two of us intending to keep those vows, including the ones about 'forsaking all others'. I intend for us to try that out, see if it works well enough for us to make it permanent. Are you willing to see how far this can go?"

"With us?" She hesitated for a minute. "You know, when you asked me out, I was imagining this as just a fling. But yes, I'm willing to try, if we move really slow. You know I had the biggest crush on you back in high school but a lot of years have gone by. I went through a lot with Frank."

"I know that, honey. Hell, I've lived in the fast lane a long time. I'm ready to slow down, find out all about the pleasures it can bring."

After that serious exchange she looked back down at him. For a minute, he thought she was looking at his scar, but realized she was examining him a bit higher, her finger grazing his pubic hair. "While I'm not into watching other people or doing those things in the video, I did like…this."

"What was it you liked, honey? Are you imagining how it would feel to have me eat your bare pussy, or how sucking my cock would feel if there weren't any hair to get in your way?"

She moved her hand back down his body and rubbed her finger over the tip of his cock, using a circular motion that had him instantly hard again. "How would it feel, Dave? I'm sure you know."

"Wanna find out? I've got clippers and a razor in the bathroom."

He liked the way her cheeks turned pink. "A friend told me she and her husband like the clean feeling…"

"Then let's do it." He'd kept his pubes shaved during offseasons because Rosa used to like it. Now that he didn't have to worry about getting razzed in locker rooms, he didn't mind going hairless again for Diane. As a matter of fact, he was downright eager. He liked eating naked pussy, and he loved fucking when neither partner had hair in the way. "Both of us, though."

"All right." She sat up, shot his scarred leg a doubtful look. "Do you need to put the brace back on?"

"No, just go over and grab that pair of crutches in the corner. I'd only be taking the brace off again as soon as we get to the bathroom." When she brought the crutches, he stood, doing his best to keep most of his weight off his knee. "Go on, honey. I'll follow you." It bothered him, having her see him as anything but fit and capable, though she'd already gotten a look at the ugly scars and she'd been seeing him use crutches away from home since he'd been back in Hedgecock.

Ego. He might not be a star quarterback anymore, and he might be moving around with a limp he wasn't sure would ever go completely away, but Dave still had some pride. Following her, he made his way into the bathroom.

Chapter Five

∞

Diane heard the thump-thump of his crutches before Dave showed up in what she'd call a playroom, not just any old bathroom. She was glad she'd had the chance to look around at the sunken hot tub he'd mentioned, with its water bubbling and churning and letting off a little steam into the chilly room. A skylight above the separate shower that was big enough for at least two people poured golden moonlight onto the slabs of creamy-veined black marble and red Texas sandstone that covered the walls and the edges of the hot tub. Dave hadn't lied. The tub really was big enough to take a swim.

The round vanity bowl, toilet and a bidet—she supposed that was what the thing by the toilet was because she'd never seen one before—were all glossy black and sparkling. Thirsty-looking ivory-colored bath sheets hung from hooks on the tile wall. There was even a massage table and what looked like a small, round stainless steel whirlpool tub like ones she'd seen in the hospital physical therapy department in Pecos, but never before in anybody's bathroom.

"Like it?" he asked, a grin on his face as he leaned hard on a crutch and took out a clipper, shave gel and razors from the top shelf of a linen closet. "We probably ought to do this in the shower since it has benches to sit on."

"Who wouldn't love it? This bathroom has to be one of your favorite places in the house. Here, let me carry the stuff." She took the supplies so he could concentrate on keeping his balance. "You really are okay with this?"

"Very okay. I'm already getting excited, just thinking about nibbling the soft, pink skin between your gorgeous legs." He paused then got into the shower, sat on one of the marble benches and adjusted the water so it sprayed just from the jets embedded about knee-high. "Come on in, the water's nice and warm. You can do me first. After we're both smooth down below, we'll take a dip in the hot tub."

She tried to hold her hand steady as she watched the clipper make quick work of his black pubic curls, leaving short stubble in its wake. Bending closer, she licked his cock. "It does look bigger."

He laughed. "Told you the hair was hiding something. Go on, get rid of all of it," he told her, lifting his good leg on the bench. Now that she had better access to his scrotum and ass, she clipped the rest of the hair off and reached for the shave gel.

When she was finished he felt smooth as a baby's butt, but not as pink because the black roots under his skin lent a dark, dangerous appearance. She loved the look—the openness it suggested went farther than the baring of his sex to her gaze. "Here, see if I've done this right." When he explored himself with one big hand, she found it strangely arousing. "Did I?"

"Oh yeah. You did good. Your turn now. Climb up here." When she did, he grabbed a handful of folded towels, put them down in front of her and slid off the bench. Carefully he knelt on the padding he'd laid. "Gotta baby the old knee. Sorry, honey." He set her legs over his shoulders and kissed her clit before starting to work.

The buzzing of the clipper had her so hot and wet, she could hardly stay still. Particularly since he kept whispering to her in a rough, sexy voice, telling her what he was doing...what he intended to do to her later. By the time he finished she was close to the edge, but he told her to hold back.

And when he lathered her up and began shaving carefully... "Oh God, I'm about to come."

"Feel free, just stay still so I won't cut your pretty pussy." When he scraped away the last of the hairs around her ass she wondered aloud, "Do some women enjoy…"

"Anal sex? Some do."

She remembered the few painful times Frank had forced her that way, shuddered. "I don't."

He set down the razor, would have bent to taste her satiny cunt except that she sounded unreasonably afraid, so he used the strength in his arms to lever himself back onto the bench beside her and spoke against her cheek. "I'm not about to force you to do anything you don't want me to. Believe that."

"Frank…"

"I'm not Frank, honey. This is me, Dave. Look at me." He held her chin, looked into her eyes. "I'll do anything to bring you pleasure. Believe that."

She turned her head, kissed his knuckles. "I want to. It's just…"

"Come on, let's get in the hot tub. It's a great place to relax while we talk." When she seemed to hesitate, he took her hand. "We need to get a few things straight."

If he could, he'd have picked Diane up and carried her the few feet to the sunken hot tub. But since he couldn't, he leaned on one crutch and wrapped his other arm around her. His ego didn't matter anymore, not when she obviously was suffering from a bunch of painful memories.

He hoped he hadn't brought those memories to life by confronting his own colorful sexual past the only way he knew how to—by being completely honest about it. As he stepped over the edge into the tub and set the crutch down, a big part of Dave wished again that Frank Granger were still alive so he could choke the life out of him. "Come on, let's see how being really naked feels."

Besides the freedom of motion he had in the water, he appreciated the fact that he could lift her, use the buoyancy of the water to make up for what he couldn't do on dry land—at least not yet. He sat across from one of the sets of Jacuzzi jets, lifted her onto his lap, facing him, and lowered her onto his cock.

"Oooh." She laid her hands on his chest, smiled.

"Feels good, doesn't it?" Damn, that was an understatement. She felt like wet silk surrounding him like a hot, arousing glove.

"Yeah. It feels great. So does the water." When she wriggled her hips, the gentle friction nearly took his breath away.

He couldn't help laughing a little. "I have to use a hot tub a lot for therapy, but I like the side benefits, too. Now tell me while we're relaxing together, what did your ex do to turn you off? I need to know so I can be careful not to do it."

She let one hand down to trail in the water, watched the bubbling waves roll over her fingers. "You sound like you want more than just a date or two and a few sessions of what I already know will be the best sex I've ever had. I want it, too, and that scares me. It's not so much the physical intimacy—I love that part. But I'm not sure about the idea of handing you the control over myself that I had to fight so hard to wrestle away from him."

"That's right, honey, I want much more than a one-night stand with you. When I saw you again it all came back—the need to have the prettiest girl in school in my arms, my bed. My hot tub. Seeing you made me want to find out not just whether we'd be good in the sack but if the emotional pull I felt was real. It is. It's too damn soon to start making lifetime vows—but for me, anyhow, my feelings are going in that direction. I want you to be my best friend, my lover. And I want us to be exclusive, the way we'll be if I'm able to persuade you that loving me won't mean you'll have to give up anything of yourself.

"I'm not into thinking that just because I love a woman, she has to become my possession—or that being her lover gives me the right to do anything except to be the only man to give her pleasure." Dave paused, considered what he'd just said. He'd always been a quick study, but he was pretty sure Diane had been in the back of his mind for years, never tasted yet lurking *there* as a hazy ideal too real to have let him dream about forever with anybody else, even Rosa. Yeah, he'd loved his wife but what he'd loved most was the fact she didn't want a level of commitment he wasn't ready to give. "To give you pleasure, honey, I need to know what I mustn't do because it will make you remember. From what little you've said, your married life was pretty miserable."

As though she were too shy to look him in the eye, Diane laid her hands on the rim of the tub on either side of Dave's head and lowered her gaze to his chest. "You've probably heard from folks in town that he got drunk and hit me. That was true. The drunker he got the meaner he became, and when the rough stock program didn't make money and he wasn't winning regularly at rodeos, he drank more."

"Why didn't you throw him out?"

"I did, eventually. I know now I should have swallowed my pride and called my mom or Keith for help. But I loved my dad and I didn't want to deprive Dylan of his. Not to mention that the idea of starting a confrontation with Frank terrified me. I guess that's why I hung on until it got so bad that it scared me more to let things go on the way they were."

It took all the self-control Dave had to listen while Diane explained some of what she'd endured sexually. The picture she painted of Frank was of a guy who, at best, didn't know the meaning of the word "foreplay" and, at worst, liked using sex as a weapon—especially the rough anal penetration she'd found degrading as well as downright painful. Sober, the man had possessed all the subtlety of a rutting bull. Drunk, he'd been a rapist—no other word for it.

Dave clenched his jaw but couldn't hold back his emotions or his words. "I wish I could have killed him for you."

"I was afraid that if I told Keith, he would have charged home and done just that. Even when he was a kid and Frank moved in at the ranch when we first married, Keith hated him. I didn't realize at the time how good my little brother's judgment was."

"I'm so sorry, honey. I can tell you this, I've never drunk to the point he apparently did. I don't foresee starting, now that I have to be an up-close role model for young boys. As I recall from my partying days, I'd laugh a lot, do silly things and pass out the minute I hit the bed, floor or whatever flat surface. I'm pretty sure it's not in me to abuse a woman or child even if I were under the influence."

"I know not all men are abusers." She lifted her head and looked him in the eye. "I know you aren't, though you're big and macho and you make me feel more helpless than Frank ever did. Helpless in a good sort of way."

"Right now I want to show you how you've got me pussy-whipped the way no woman ever has before but first I promise you this—I'll never, ever use my size and strength to make you do anything you don't want to do, sexually or otherwise. Or my money," he added when he thought about how wealth apparently intimidated her.

She smiled, wriggled her bare cunt against his balls. "Somehow I doubt you'd have to force me. I love the way you make love with me." Her expression turned serious and she slid her arms around him. "I've been fucked hundreds of times, but tonight's the first time I've made love."

"You have no idea how good it makes me feel to hear that." Her admission stroked his ego, left him feeling as invincible as he used to after having a good game. "We're gonna make love a lot. When we wake up tomorrow morning, I want you to be snuggled in my arms. We'll go over to your place and feed your animals then spend the day in town. I'm anxious to show you off, not to mention there's a meeting I'm supposed to attend about the reunion. We'll have lunch at the café."

Dave felt the tension in her body lessen as he rubbed up and down her spine and the swirling waters surrounded them, a warm, wet cocoon that bound them together as tightly as any vow. As tightly as his sex was buried in hers, for a while he was content to stay there, not moving, savoring a connection more spiritual than sexual. He'd never felt closer to another woman, or so content to let his emotions have free rein.

"All right," she said as she broke out in a brilliant smile. "Meanwhile, let's make love and make the most of this time while Dylan's away."

* * * * *

"You said you wanted more togetherness, to take this to the next level. I'm still a little freaked at the idea. Want to paint me a clearer picture about where you see this going?" Diane stretched out beside him once they'd climbed out of the tub, cleansed themselves on the bidet he had shown her how to use, dried off and adjourned to his bed. The incredibly soft sheets brushed her sensitized flesh while he stroked her with a slow, sensuous rhythm.

"Yeah, I want you here with me every day and night. It may sound crazy but I already want to be exclusive. I want to be the one who takes care of you, not because I'm a possessive asshole like Frank. That doesn't mean I don't have a bit of a jealous streak where you're concerned. The idea of you making love with another man makes me see red, sort of like Bullyboy seems to get whenever he sees me."

When he gave her a half-chuckle, Diane was surprised that the statement as well as the way he said it made her feel warm in all the right places. Not afraid, the way she'd been of Frank's jealous rages.

Dave stroked his hand along her spine. "I don't want to scare you, but I can imagine asking you to marry me a little way down the road, Diane, if we both decide we want this. It seems soon, I know, but I've reached the point in my life that I know what's real and what's not. What I'm feeling for you is real. I'll give you all the time you need. But will you at least give it some consideration?"

It took her a moment to digest his words but she wanted this as much as he did. "Yes, I'll think about it. But what if Dylan doesn't…" Suddenly needing space, she rolled onto her side facing the nightstand.

Dave followed her, curling around her like a big, warm spoon. "He likes me. And he seems like a good kid who'd want his mom happy. Do I make you happy?"

His hard, thick sex lay in the crease between her thighs, reminding her how she'd come three times — three times more than she had in the previous forty years of her life — in one incredible night. He had one strong arm around her, his touch protective as well as arousing. "Yes. You make me happier than I've ever been."

"You know, I'm pretty damn sure I've been half in love with you since high school. Timing was wrong for us then. I didn't want to have to look at Edie's sad eyes the way I'd have had to if I broke up with her before we graduated. So I took the easy way and waited until I was going away to college." He paused, looked away as though he hated to admit the rest.

Then he met her gaze, his expression pained. "To be honest, I wanted the hell out of you my entire last year of high school, and if I hadn't been scared of fighting Frank I'd have broken up with Edie and done my best to get you away from him. I was a fucking coward, and because of it, I floated around in a sexual limbo for too damn long. And you had a miserable marriage to a bully I should have put in his place."

"He'd have hurt you, and that would have nearly killed me." Diane recalled the boys Frank had beaten, regretted that she'd once seen his jealousy as proof that he loved her. "Not that you weren't plenty big and strong, but he had a mean streak worse than the wild bull that finally killed him."

"I should have found him and taken him apart limb from limb as soon as I was old enough and strong enough. I could have done it by the time I finished my first year of college."

"You didn't—and I married him like a crazy kid who wanted somebody to take care of me after Daddy died. We can't change the past. Only the future."

Dave took her hand, held it as though he'd never let her go. Yet she felt no force, just gentle persuasion. "Do you love me, honey?"

"Yes." She did. She probably had kept that flame going in the back of her mind for longer than she dared admit. "I love you."

"And I love you, too. I'll love you the rest of my life. I promise."

Diane trusted his word. No man who'd tell the truth about his sexual past when lies would have definitely served him better would lie about something as important to him as love. "I believe you. And I believe I'll never love another man the way I love you."

"Then let's take the plunge since we're both sure. We have kids to consider, ones I'm not anxious to have wondering when or if we're going to make it legal. Marry me. Come live with me here. You've worked too damn hard for too long. Let me take care of you and Dylan, and help me raise my kids when they're with us."

Diane's head was spinning. She'd known Dave when they were youngsters, heard a lot about his exploits while he was gone. Now she was deep in lust and certain she loved the man he'd become. "I don't know. What about my place, the animals? Aside from the fact that this place has all the creature comforts, I'd never feel comfortable making love with you where I lived with Frank."

When Dave spoke, his damp breath tickled her ear. "The animals aren't a problem. I have a contractor scheduled to come next month and fix up the barn and fencing. I intend to buy a horse or two for DJ and Cathy to ride when they visit and maybe one for me when my knee's in good enough shape for me to ride. Meanwhile we can drive over to your place every day and take care of Bullyboy and your horses."

One by one, Dave countered her arguments, and by the time the sun started shedding light on them through windows near the ceiling, Diane figured out what really mattered. She loved Dave and he loved her. They belonged together. All the obstacles, all the mindless details would work themselves out. For too many years she'd stood alone, now she'd stand with her strong, gentle lover. Together they'd guide her son and his two children for the few years until they'd go on their own, make their own lives.

"Dave?"

He stirred, cupped her bare sex in one big hand. "Yeah, honey?"

"I'll marry you unless my son has awfully strong objections."

"You won't be sorry, honey. I'll see to it." Nudging her rear hole with his erection, he bent and whispered in her ear. "I love you, too, more than I've ever loved another human being."

He stroked her, his touch light, not the least bit threatening. "You said you didn't like anal sex but I bet you will if it's done the right way. Are you game to try it, with me?" His motion easy, deliberate, he rubbed the tip of his cock around her rim.

"I'm not sure."

When he nuzzled her throat, he sent chills of anticipation all through her body. "It feels good when you play with me there. I don't know…"

"Let's find out. Reach over in the drawer and fish out another condom. There's a tube of lubricant in there, too. Grab it, please. God, baby, I hate that I can't do everything I want to do with you but think positive. My knee will heal, eventually. And as it does, the sex will get even better."

Diane was sorry his knee was messed up but glad to be starting out this way with him, knowing there were limits to what he could and couldn't do with her. She rolled over, found his huge, naked sex and stroked it with wonder while he moaned with obvious pleasure. She bent and kissed away the lubrication from his tip then moved lower, licked his velvety-smooth ball sac. Then, although she couldn't help being a little doubtful about taking him anally, she wanted to try because she trusted him not to hurt her—at least not much. Her fingers shaking just a little bit, she slid the condom on him. Opening the lube, she applied it over his turgid length.

"My turn." She turned, offered the tube of lubricant as she presented him her ass.

"Tell me if my scratchy chin hurts your pussy," he said, making a sweep along her smooth inner lips from her swollen clit to her vagina. His tongue slid, its wetness mingling with her own juices. Finally he kissed the sensitive tissue around her rim, only pressing his lubed finger past the tight sphincter muscle when she begged him for more.

She loved the feel of his early morning beard on her most intimate places. Knowing they'd cleansed each other thoroughly alleviated the queasiness she'd thought she might feel, preparing to participate in an act she used to fear and dread. "Do you want me to roll off you and get up on my hands and knees?"

"No, honey, this is gonna be your show. Climb on top of me, only this time you'll be getting a great view of my fucked-up knee that wouldn't like it at all if we did this doggie-style. I'll hold your butt in my hands to guide you down on me, but I want you to stop anytime you feel the least bit of discomfort. If you want to, you can play with my balls. God, yeah, I love how your hands feel on me."

The lube felt cold when he positioned the broad head of his cock at her rear entrance. "Come on down, you'll feel pressure as you let me in the door."

Pressure? More like excruciating pain but she didn't want to stop. She wanted to give him this, as she'd given him the rest of herself. Tears burned her cheeks as she made herself concentrate on his muscular, lightly furred thighs, the horrible scar on his knee, until suddenly the pain lessened. She felt a not-unpleasant fullness but also the smooth heat of his testicle sac nestled next to her pussy, a delicious friction where his perineum kissed her clit. When he let go of her ass cheeks and began playing with her breasts and nipples, a hard, fast climax overtook her.

"That's it, honey, see how good it can be?" He sounded tortured, as though holding back his own climax. "Quick, get off me and take off the condom and give me your precious pussy."

It was hours later and a noonday sun was beating down on the room when Diane remembered how great it had felt when Dave had come inside her, burst after hot burst of steamy fluid. She'd reveled in it, curled up next to him and slept...

"Dave?"

He stretched, pulled her back in his arms. "Yeah, honey?"

"What would you do if I accidentally got pregnant?"

He laughed. "It wouldn't be an accident. It would be a gift I hope we'd both cherish. Rosa and I waited a few years before starting on a baby. You and I don't have that much time left if we're gonna make one or two of our own."

"No, we don't. And I wouldn't mind having your baby at all. But, darling, I'd really like for people not to count the months, so you'll need to use those condoms until after we get married. Let's just hope we're not already too late."

"No. But I will promise we'll get married very soon so at least the gossips will have to count almost all the way to nine. Give me a quickie and then we'll get up and take care of business."

She couldn't tell him no, so she snuggled up at his side, draping one leg over his hip and holding onto him as he entered her slowly, gently, as though she were precious, fragile. She wouldn't always want it this way but now it felt right. A benediction and a promise Diane could trust...now and forever.

Epilogue
A week later, and a week before the reunion

೫

The last place Dave would have thought he'd get married was in Hedgecock's only café, but its owner had offered the place to Diane for free—and she'd accepted. He had trouble getting used to her frugal nature, but he understood the pride that hadn't let her take help from Keith or her mom.

She damn well would take from him now that he'd just slid a plain gold band next to the hefty diamond solitaire he'd put there Wednesday, as soon as FedEx had delivered it from Tiffany's Dallas store. She'd practically refused it and probably would have if Dylan hadn't commented that it wasn't all that much bigger than the one Uncle Keith had given Tina. While Dave enjoyed seeing his woman decked out in diamonds by the pound, he also liked her lack of avarice that he'd encountered from a few gold-digging bimbos. Sitting at a table by the dance floor, he watched the lights reflect off that rock while Diane danced with Mel's son Bobby.

Big ego. Yeah, he had one, probably always would even now that having a healthy one wasn't a necessity for his profession anymore. He'd never admit it to a soul, but he knew deep down that part of the reason he'd gone for the big bling was that he didn't want his wife's ring overshadowed by the jewelry he'd noticed the other quarterbacks' wives were wearing. Someday he was going to have to lose the fierce sense of competition, or at least tone it down. But not now. He'd caught the best partner of the bunch and he was damn proud of it.

God, did he love her! Dave followed her with his gaze as she danced with the rookie while Bobby's wife chatted with her mother-in-law. Tina and Keith danced, too, but Dave was too happy to let himself be bummed because he was the only one too banged up to hit the dance floor.

At his bride's insistence, Daisy was here, sporting a fresh puppy cut and decked out in pale-blue bows on her pompoms. So were Cathy and DJ, accompanied by their mother, a wonderful surprise Diane had kept from him until an hour before the wedding. The kids seemed to be taking it all in stride, Dave thought, looking over by the buffet table to see them all chowing down on barbecued beef and baked beans. From the look of it, they seemed to be competing to see who could sneak the most treats to the delighted dog.

"Good luck, Dave, you deserve it." Rosa set her plate on the table and bent to kiss his cheek. "We had a lot of good times but they were bound to end. Maybe I'll be as lucky as you, second time around."

"I hope so. You'll always have a big spot in my heart. Thanks for coming and bringing the kids. It means a lot to both of us."

Bobby walked Diane back to Dave. "Thanks, old man, for letting me dance with your gorgeous bride. Diane and I go way back." The kid's grin took the bite off his words.

Diane laughed as she sat and laid her left hand on top of Dave's braced knee. "We go back so far, I used to change your diaper. Go on now, your wife's looking lonely over there." She turned to Rosa. "I'm so glad you're here."

"I'm glad, too, that I had an open weekend. DJ and Cathy would have had fits if they couldn't have come to their daddy's wedding, but I'm sure neither of us would have wanted them to fly by themselves and change planes." She grinned. "I imagined you and Diane would have better things to do than make a long drive to collect them in San Antonio. Dave, I'm surprised Colin isn't here."

"Mel said he'd be arriving in a day or so. He's driving from Savannah, stopping to audition a couple of rookie free agents along the way. Why don't you stay, enjoy the reunion with us? I'm sure Mel would jump at the chance of having you on the program opening night."

"I wish I could but it would look strange. Besides, the kids have to be back in school on Monday. I doubt the headmaster would be too happy if they missed ten days. I am going to send them here for the summer, though, if you two don't mind. Mother's getting too cranky to deal with their antics while I go on tour."

Dave looked over at Diane, saw her look of genuine pleasure. "That's the best wedding present you could give us, Rosa." Weddings didn't have to mean formal gowns and thousand-dollar wines served from crystal fountains. This one, with its barbecue and beer and side dishes guests had contributed, was good enough. Better than good enough. He stood and brought Diane up next to him when Cal Tate proposed the wedding toast.

Later, in their bed after Keith and Tina took Dylan to her old place and Rosa dragged DJ and Cathy to the hotel with a delighted Daisy, Diane watched moonlight bounce off the embarrassingly huge diamond on her hand as she stroked her husband's beautiful, delicious cock before bending and sucking on one of his nipples. "Your ex is gorgeous. Nice, too. Do you still want...are you still attracted to her?"

"No. Like I told Rosa, I'll always care for her as a friend and my kids' mom. But I love you and only want to make love with you. Tonight I'm gonna do it right. To hell with my knee."

"But Dave..."

"Don't worry, I'll leave the brace on but I've got to..." Rolling her to her back, he spread her legs, lay between them and buried his face in her wet heat until she squirmed with wanting him. When he finally raised his head, her juices glistened on his lips and chin as he looped both arms around her calves and lifted them onto his broad shoulders. "You're so fucking beautiful and I love you more than I ever thought I could love anybody."

With that he sank deep into her welcoming heat, in control yet never threatening the way she'd worried he might be when he took a dominant position. He moved in her, long and deep and delicious, slick flesh on slick, naked flesh.

As another orgasm racked her body she opened her eyes, saw her hands framing his beloved face as he began to come inside her. Her ring sparkled in the moonlight, illuminating his features as he claimed her with burst after burst of hot semen. She knew then. It was the spirit, not the price of his gifts, that she'd always savor.

She loved Dave Delaney with all her heart.

The End

COACH ME

80

Trademarks Acknowledgement

ඏ

The author acknowledges the trademarked status and trademark owners of the following wordmarks mentioned in this work of fiction:

Corona: Cerveceria Modela, S.A. de C.V.

Gatorade: Stokely-Van Camp, Inc.

Little League: Little League Baseball, Inc.

NFL, NFL Network: NFL Enterprises LLC

Pee Wee football: American Youth Football, Inc.

Pillsbury Dough Boy: Pillsbury Company

Porsche: Dr. Ing. h. c. f. Porsche Aktiengesellschaft Corporation

Super Bowl: National Football League unincorporated association

Author's Notes and Glossary

ౠ

I'm a rabid football fan, or rather a rabid fan of several generations of quarterbacks I've watched play on TV and in person. This fandom caused me to come up with an idea for the *Gridiron Lovers*, a series of erotic romances about four star quarterbacks who just happened to have grown up in the same small west Texas town and who went on to fame and fortune as professionals. All of these guys and their teams are fictional, and any resemblance to an actual NFL player or team past or present is purely coincidental.

The four books' titles apparently need some explanation for readers who haven't been watching games every fall since…well, for quite a few years. Suffice it to say, I've watched every Super Bowl since number three, when Broadway Joe Namath came through on his guarantee of a win for the New York Jets. I was just a baby then (wink-wink).

So here we go. Mind you, these definitions may not all be technically correct, since they're based on my personal observations and comments I've digested from the media personalities who call the games on TV every Sunday from August through December and early January. Take a minute and read these pages first, so you won't become totally confused.

Naked Bootleg. This is a play where the quarterback takes the snap, fakes a handoff to a running back but keeps the ball. He runs the opposite direction from the runner without a lineman protecting him—this makes the bootleg "naked"— and either passes to a receiver downfield or runs downfield himself. I thought it was a great play for Bobby Anthony to make during his first NFL appearance, as well as a sexy-sounding title for the first *Gridiron Lovers* book.

Forward Pass. The quarterback drops back from the line of scrimmage and throws the ball forward to an eligible receiver downfield. Eligible receivers, I think, are the backs, tight ends and wide receivers. Keith Connors is a master of the forward pass on the field, but he's pretty hot in the bedroom, as well.

Clutch, as in *Hot in the Clutch.* A player, usually a quarterback, who's especially good at coming through with points when the team needs them most. Dave Delaney's career is almost over, but he can still be counted on for a great play in the clutch, whether it's on the field or in a woman's bed.

Coach, as in *Coach Me.* The masterminds of the game, often former players — great or average. Each team has several coaches, with the "head coach" in charge of it all. Colin Zanardi's playing days are over, but he's still in the game, not only with his team but also with the hottest of the local ladies.

Now for the glossary, which I'm putting in alphabetical order so you can refer to it as needed while you read:

Athletic waivers: a certain number of exceptions a college coach can use to recruit top athletes who don't meet minimum academic standards for the institution which are determined by a combination of high school grades and standardized test scores.

Audible: when the quarterback calls out a change of the play at the line of scrimmage.

Block: what linemen do to keep defensive players away from the quarterback, as in "throw a block" or "miss a block".

Center: the player on the offensive line who snaps the ball to the quarterback when he's "under center" or "in the shotgun".

Clipboard: the object that all backup quarterbacks almost always have in their hands while standing on the sidelines; a backup quarterback's assignment, as in "carry the clipboard".

Depth chart: a chart that shows each player's status at his position — starter, second string, third string, etc.

Double coverage: two defensive players are covering (chasing) one potential receiver for the offense at the same time.

Field position: the spot on the hundred-yard field where the ball is spotted — the closer to the defense's goal, the better the field position is for the offense.

First down: when the offense starts a series or moves ten yards down the field toward the opponent's goal — can be a longer or shorter distance if penalties are involved — and is then given four more tries to make another ten yards or a touchdown, or kick the ball away.

Fumble: when the football gets loose from whatever player had it in his hands and is fair game for any player, either offensive or defensive, to pick up and claim — called a fumble recovery.

Groupie: a woman who's obsessed with professional athletes and wants any athlete, but preferably a star, for a day or night's fun and games.

Handoff: when the quarterback takes the snap from the center and immediately hands it to a running back.

Huddle: a gathering of the entire offense around the quarterback, who gives them the play the coach has sent from the sideline or via a speaker in the quarterback's helmet.

Interception: when an opposing player catches a pass, thereby causing the defense to get the ball.

Linebackers: defensive players who often break through the offensive line and go after the quarterback (there are three of them in some defenses, four in others); they also break up pass plays downfield by stopping the receivers who are trying to catch passes and/or get additional yards after catching the ball.

Line of scrimmage: the point on the football field where the ball is placed.

Nose tackle: a defensive player who lines up in front of the center, usually a huge beast of a man who opens up holes in the offense so other defensive players can get to the quarterback (Note: this assumes the defense is what's called a three-four where the nose tackle and two defensive ends line up in front, with four linebackers behind them—the setup is different, although I can't explain how, if the defense is a so-called four-three with two tackles and two defensive ends in front and three linebackers behind them).

Penalty: a misdeed on the part of an offensive or defensive player that causes the team to be penalized from five to fifteen yards, and sometimes—in the case of a penalty on the defense—to create an automatic first down for the offense. Some of the reasons penalties are imposed are for holding, roughing the passer, unnecessary roughness, illegal motion before the ball is snapped, extra man on the field, or illegal formation.

Pick-six: an interception that the defensive player runs back for a touchdown.

Punt: kick on fourth down, so the opposing team will get the ball as far as possible downfield; *punter*: the player who kicks punts.

Receiver, or wide receiver: an offensive player whose main function is to catch passes from the quarterback.

Running back: offensive player who takes handoffs from the quarterback and runs the ball, or who catches short passes "out of the backfield" and then runs for yardage.

Sack: when a defensive player gets to the quarterback before he passes the ball and throws him to the ground.

Scout team: a team of non-starting players who study and then try to duplicate the plays of an opposing team while the first team practices against them during the week before the actual game (the backup quarterback usually runs the scout team, although sometimes that job goes to the third-string guy).

Shotgun: a formation where the quarterback stands a good distance back from the center to take the snap.

Snap: the movement of the ball from the center to the quarterback.

Taking a knee: when the quarterback takes the snap and goes down on one knee instead of initiating a play as the time is winding down to zero at halftime or at the end of a game.

Three-and-out: an expression that describes an offensive series where the offense goes three snaps without getting a first down.

Tight end: offensive players who generally line up at the ends of the offensive line (if there are two of them in for the play) and who block as well as catch passes.

Turnover: the offense gives the ball to the other team because of a fumble or interception rather than after three-and-out or a touchdown.

I hope you all enjoy this series as much as I've loved putting it together. *Naked Bootleg* started it all, and it's the only book that takes place during football season, so you won't see a lot of actual playing—at least on the field—in the rest of the series.

Kick back now and enjoy *Coach Me,* the story of the hometown reunion that brings all four players back to their roots and pairs the hot, submissive reunion organizer with the former NFL star who started the tradition of Hedgecock developing generations of great pro quarterbacks.

Prologue

ඝ

He might be the oldest of the Hedgecock signal callers the town would honor at the reunion next week, but he looked incredibly hot to her. For at least the hundredth time she stared at the publicity photo the Rebels had sent. The deep, decisive sound of his voice still reverberated in her ear from their latest phone conversation moments earlier.

Susan Anderson picked up the glossy eight-by-ten, traced the strong jaw, the neck that looked muscular yet not muscle bound. Yeah, Colin Zanardi deserved his spot on the cover of the souvenir program she'd just gotten back from the printer in Pecos. She loved the way his curly dark-brown hair was liberally sprinkled with silver. She fantasized that it would feel crisp against her fingers, the curl tamed by a short, no-nonsense cut.

She imagined his expressive brown eyes would turn almost black with desire. His stern-looking mouth would curve in a feral grin, and he'd tell her what he wanted from her in that voice that brooked no disobedience. Just thinking about the fact he'd be here Sunday, not just in Hedgecock but here in her house, had her pussy wet with anticipation.

Not just for a quick scratch of the itch that had driven her since her Master died two years ago. But for more.

She didn't know how she could tell from a handful of photos and a few long-distance phone conversations with the man, but she knew. Colin was a sexual Dominant or damn close to it—one who thrived on being in control. Every time they'd talked, she'd sensed more strongly that he'd drive her to the kind of sexual satisfaction she hadn't experienced for more than two years though God only knew how hard she'd tried to find it.

* * * * *

You'll be staying at my house. The reunion's got every hotel within two hundred miles booked solid.

Colin Zanardi leaned back in his desk chair at the Rebels' Savannah headquarters. He'd obviously been too damn busy lately. Otherwise he wouldn't have been half hard, wondering if Susan Anderson were as soft and submissive as she sounded on the phone.

During the last few phone calls they'd shared, the sexy widow had clearly been making a play for him. That didn't surprise him—a good many groupie types still wanted a piece of him even though he'd hung up his cleats thirteen years ago and moved over to the coaching side of football. What intrigued him was the element of raw need he heard in her voice each time they'd spoken and the hint of feminine submissiveness that appealed so strongly to his dominant nature.

For the first time since agreeing to take part in this reunion, Colin found himself actually looking forward to his first return to the tiny west Texas town since he'd graduated from high school almost thirty-two years ago.

Closing his eyes, he tried to dredge a picture of Susan from his damn near nonexistent memories of his high school years. Hell, that wasn't going to work. She'd probably changed her name when she married. Besides, since she mentioned being a former classmate of recently retired Rebels quarterback Dave Delaney, she'd have been a child when he was a teenager.

To tell the truth, Colin didn't even recall the kids he'd gone to classes with, other than having vague memories of a teammate or two, and a couple girls whose pussies he remembered better than their faces.

So Susan was about ten years Colin's junior. Not exactly his contemporary but a hell of a lot closer to it than the giggly twenty-something groupie he'd fucked a couple months ago after the Rebels had won the division championship. The woman hadn't complained. She'd given every indication that she'd enjoyed him immensely. But after the deed was done he'd felt like a dirty old man. Since then he'd pretty much limited himself to playing at the club every once in a while with the unattached subs who worked there.

When they'd spoken on the phone earlier about Dave's upcoming wedding, Dave had mentioned Susan, hinted that she was basically a slut. But Colin hadn't gotten that impression from her during their occasional chats they'd been having since the reunion plans had been developing. Yeah, she'd been hitting on him, sort of. Maybe it was wishful thinking on his part, but he thought Susan might be a sexual submissive in desperate need of a dominant man, not just an aging groupie hungry for sex.

His balls tightened. His cock swelled painfully against the zipper of his jeans. For a long time he sat there conjuring various sexual scenarios he hoped would come to fruition next Sunday when he arrived in Hedgecock — at Susan's house.

Chapter One
Home for the reunion

ઈ૦

Funny, Colin didn't remember a thing he'd seen the past half hour, except this junction of two blacktop roads and a square sandstone hotel with its carefully tended hedges and gardens. A photographer had set up in that garden to take pictures of his classmates at his senior prom.

Strange snippet to recall since Colin couldn't bring to mind the girl he'd escorted that night. Not her name or her face, or even whether he'd scored once the dance had ended. His three years at Hedgecock High had sped by, leaving him with few memories except for a vague feeling that he hadn't quite belonged there, that he'd been considered more a strong arm who could throw a football than a living, breathing part of the tiny community.

He hadn't been able to pack up and leave for college quickly enough once he had his diploma and his scholarship. And he'd never thought he'd be coming back someday. Not coming home, because Hedgecock had been just a stopping point in the journey between childhood and independence.

He paused at the crossroad, wondered why the hell he'd agreed to come back now, thirty-two years later, when he could as easily have written a large check to help the struggling community renovate the field where he'd played. He might have saved himself what could end up being an uncomfortable journey down memory lane.

Unlike Dave, who'd occasionally returned to see the grandmother who raised him and who now owned the small ranch where he'd grown up, Colin had no family calling him back to Hedgecock. No family period, except his old man who'd done his duty and taken him on after his mom died, and who still followed the call of black gold, most recently in an oilfield near a Mississippi town with the improbable name of Soso.

Early in life, Colin had learned it hurt too much to look back. So he'd focused clearly on the present, even more so on his future. Still, being back in west Texas where he'd gotten to know the man who'd sired him made him wonder...

Maybe he'd detour by that oilfield on the way back to Savannah and say hello. After all, the last time he'd seen his father had been in New Orleans before the Super Bowl earlier that year where they'd wolfed down coffee and beignets in the French Quarter. They were hardly anybody's idea of the ideal family — but Zeke Zanardi had stepped in after Colin's mom and stepdad died in an accident and kept Colin out of foster care when he was fourteen. And through all the years since then, the two had maintained a loose connection that neither had ever tried to tighten — maybe for fear of severing the tenuous relationship altogether.

Colin's family was his football team, whichever one he owed allegiance to for any given year. For fifteen years he'd felt the family connection more clearly while he'd been married to his team owner's daughter, but that connection had always been palpable, from the years he spent here through college and as a player in the NFL. Only recently had he started feeling the Rebels were a lousy substitute for relationships that outlasted contracts and seasons, regretting he'd opted to make football pretty much his whole life.

So here he was, back where it all had started. Memories of the years between then and now bombarded his brain in bits and pieces. Maybe he'd come back because he needed to face his past, understand who he was and why.

Don't kid yourself, Zanardi. The reason you're here is because you need to see if the woman who's put together this reunion matches the voice that's been echoing in your head since the first time she called and asked you to do this reunion thing.

Colin shifted into gear, headed down the road toward Hedgecock, toward the seductive, submissive-sounding woman whose voice had lured him where he'd sworn he'd never go again.

* * * * *

If she were a man, people would call her a sexual predator.

Dave's chuckling assessment crossed Colin's mind when he arrived at Susan Anderson's cobbled-sandstone bungalow, his bag in hand. Other than an older sedan he spotted in the detached garage, his own vintage black Porsche coupe, coated with west Texas dust from the road and parked in front of her house, was the only vehicle on the otherwise deserted block. She'd mentioned something about holding a meeting tonight about the football camp and reunion taking place the following week, but he didn't see any signs that anybody else might be inside.

He lifted the old-fashioned doorknocker and let it fall with a sharp thud. In a few seconds the door opened, framing the prettiest, sexiest-looking woman Colin had seen in a long, long time.

She greeted him with a big hug, unusual since they were practically strangers yet anything but off-putting. Her body felt good against his—soft yet firm—and she smelled of something slightly tart, a little bit flowery. He liked it, whatever it was.

"Come on in and make yourself at home," she said, holding the door open and motioning him inside. "Your room is this way."

He liked her soft-spoken, west-Texas drawl—more honest than the syrupy Savannah accents he'd been hearing the past five years and a hell of a lot sexier than the clipped East Coast speech he'd become used to during the sixteen years he'd lived in the Big Apple. Dark-haired and a knockout from head to toe, she had a mouth that would perfectly surround a man's cock.

She looked younger than he'd imagined. Not as young as a twenty-something groupie, of course. But well-preserved, with beautiful skin kissed but not baked by the fierce west Texas sun. He found her incredibly desirable.

He followed her down a hallway to what obviously was the master bedroom with a small adjoining bath. It wasn't where she slept, because the disuse was evident in spite of the smell of furniture polish and freshly laundered linens, and the bowl full of spring flowers on top of the old-fashioned dresser. The bed itself looked comfortable, not unlike those in the hotels he'd stayed in during his week-long trips to colleges to check out potential draftees. Not a bad layout, considering the alternative, which would have been a motor home he'd considered renting for the week before she'd suggested he stay here. "This looks great. Thanks for letting me bunk in with you."

"No problem. You can unpack if you like."

"I'll do that later." Colin wanted to stay with her, see if his first impression had hit the mark.

"Fine. Come with me. You've got to be hungry after that long drive." She showed him to the living room they'd passed by when he arrived. "You can wait in here while I get you some snacks."

When she left him, he looked around. Not so much at furniture that had seen a lot of years' use as at the sensual feast she'd created.

A sweet, musky smell of burning incense swirled around his head, caught on the gentle breeze from a lazily turning ceiling fan. Colin remembered that smell, found it as arousing now as he had years ago when he'd first smelled it when he entered a posh dungeon on the upper West Side for the first time. For years he'd played sex games there every Tuesday—

as long as he'd been throwing footballs the previous weekends in the Jersey Meadowlands.

The frankly sexual ambiance had Colin's nerves on edge. Not to mention what it was doing to his libido. Nothing was going to happen, though, at least not right away, if Susan had been serious about having a meeting tonight about the reunion activities. He imagined they'd have company soon. Probably not Dave, who'd just gotten married on Saturday. But Keith Connors and Bobby Anthony, the other Hedgecock High School signal callers who'd followed Colin to the NFL, would surely be at this meeting to go over details for the football camp and reunion activities scheduled for the coming week. And others who'd worked on plans for the football camp and other activities probably would show up, as well.

Colin imagined his seduction, if that were what Susan had in mind and it looked as though it was, wouldn't happen until later. Then he noticed a small, round table in an alcove framed with floor-to-ceiling windows. Set for two with a white linen tablecloth, pastel-patterned china and gleaming silverware, the table was bathed in orange-gold light from the sunset pouring through the windows. His gaze settled on a long-stemmed red rose that lay across one plate, its thorns standing out prominently against the creamy porcelain. Odd that the flower was presented that way instead of in a vase in the middle of the table the way one would expect.

But that place went not to a floral arrangement in a silver or fine china bowl, but to a fat white novena candle in a tall, round glass container, the cheap kind they sold in every mom-and-pop store in this part of the country. The candle container sat in a sturdy, black metal holder. The fact that the container held the type of low-heat, cheap paraffin candle often used in BDSM play didn't escape Colin's notice, and he glanced again at the rose, paying closer attention this time. As he suspected, Susan had stripped its leaves away, leaving the thorns accessible.

No one else was coming. His hostess had set this party up for two and done it in a way that left no doubt in Colin's mind that she wanted him to dominate her sexually. His cock rose faster than it had in years. If, as he now believed, she was a sexual submissive searching for a Dom to fulfill her needs, then he was just the man to oblige her.

* * * * *

Was he the Dom she'd been dreaming of since she'd first heard his compelling, sexy voice on the phone last fall? Susan stood in the kitchen, breathing hard. In the flesh, Colin Zanardi was every bit as hot as he'd appeared in the head shot the Rebels' PR department had sent for her to use to promote the reunion. Unlike the info sheets she'd gotten for the other three Hedgecock quarterbacks who'd gone pro, the one for Colin had left off vital statistics like height, weight, and so on. That information wasn't pertinent for coaches, she guessed, but she was happy to have learned when he showed up at her door that he was tall enough for her to rest her head on his broad, muscular chest, and as hard and apparently fit as most men twenty years younger.

The man himself had been lost in local legend over the years. Susan had interviewed practically everyone in town who might have known Colin back in the day. It had surprised her that not even his classmates had seemed able to provide much in the way of personal anecdotes, although most had followed his successful NFL career on TV. They'd been able to tell her Colin had been a Super Bowl MVP but not what he'd done off the field or who had been his friends when they were kids. Apparently he'd been a loner who'd drifted into town just as he was starting high school and had just as suddenly gone away.

Susan didn't care. She was interested in Colin now, not in what he might have been thirty years ago when she'd been more interested in playing with dolls than with boys. If she hadn't known better, and if it hadn't been for his graying hair and the deep laugh lines etched around his dark eyes, she'd have thought he was around her own age, not ten years older.

She'd give his chiseled lips an "A" for kissability. She'd fallen in lust with his picture but he was so much hotter in the flesh. And compelling. He'd only been here a half hour but already she felt his presence—sensed his dominance. Yeah. The man was not only hot but brimming over with self-confidence. The sort of self-control she craved in a man.

Her pulse raced with anticipation. Would he recognize the signs she'd laid out? And if he saw significance in the rose, the candle or the incense, would he say something about them? She hoped he'd guess what it was she needed so desperately—what she hoped he'd want to provide.

Some of the Rebels' players who'd come to town for Dave's wedding and were staying to help out at the football camp next week had been talking last night at the café. From snippets of conversation Susan had overheard she guessed Colin might be the "boss" they'd talked about who liked to join in sex games at the private club called Necessary Roughness. She hoped so because she wanted him to play with her.

Maybe she'd gone too far with the blatant hints. But damn it, her Master had been dead for two years. She missed the sexual games they used to play, even the ones that hurt. Especially those. Her gaze wandered briefly to the closed door that led downstairs to a room that used to house a torture chamber with imaginatively crafted toys she'd had hauled away after Donnie's death. No one would guess now that the room had ever housed anything other than a storm cellar and a cool, dry storeroom for emergency provisions.

That room was her past, a part of her that lay buried in a thick coat of west Texas dust, a silent shrine to Donnie Anderson and what he'd meant to her. To the fact that no matter how many men she'd fucked since he'd been gone— and there had been a lot of them—she'd felt vaguely dissatisfied after leaving each one, like a dedicated chocoholic given nothing to feast on but vanilla ice cream.

Hopeful tonight would be different, she found the remote for the stereo and started her favorite music DVD. She adjusted the sound—not too loud, just a subtle background for seduction. Opening the refrigerator, she took out the plate of finger foods she'd arranged earlier. Not knowing her guest's taste in beverages, she set a bottle of Corona and one of spring water in an ice bucket and put the bucket onto the tray with the food.

* * * * *

Mellow, sexy music, the beat slow but strong and suggestive of a languid fucking session, filled Colin's ears as Susan came back in the front room with a tray full of food and drink. Her purple dress clung to her slender but curvy body, soft and inviting as it swirled around the prettiest bare legs he'd ogled in a long time. When she bent to set the tray on the table the dress caught in the crack of her nicely rounded ass.

No underwear. His breath caught in his throat and blood slammed into his groin.

She stood before him now, her hands clasped behind her back, head bowed in a classic pose of submission. He lowered his gaze to her full, firm breasts, the hard nubs of the nipples prominent beneath the clingy material. "What do you want, Susan?"

"You, Sir. I want you to take me, let me pleasure you."

He noted the way she addressed him then eyed the food. "Feed me," he said, grasping her chin and raising her head until he looked into her eyes that were almost black with need. "But first, tell me how deep you're into this game."

She held his gaze, smiled. "As deep as you want me to be, Sir."

With one finger he traced around her slender neck. Soft. Her skin felt like the silk scarves he might use later to bind her.

"What if I wanted to lead you around town on a leash in front of everybody?" That had been a stopping point with Elise, who'd insisted he confine flaunting his ownership to the clubs and inside the Upper West Side condo that had been their home.

"I'd hope this could stay between us, but I'd follow your command…Master."

He was ready to play her game, if for no other reason than it had been a long time—too long—since he'd played with a true submissive, and she was nothing if not the most desirable woman who'd offered herself to him this way in recent memory. "Know that what I want is your pleasure, whatever it takes. If you need pain, I'll oblige you. I'm more into the mental elements of dominance, though."

Glancing over at the rose, he picked it up and brushed the petals across her cheek before raking the thorny stem lightly over her throat and shoulders, being careful not to draw blood. He noticed how her breathing became shallow and her pulse started to race at the touch of the sharp thorns to her naked skin. He smelled the female musk that rose from her cunt.

Yeah, she was into pain. More importantly, she was eager to be dominated. Colin's cock throbbed with anticipation. "Feed me."

Her motion deliberate, practiced, she dipped each shrimp into a creamy pink sauce then fed it to him, her fingers lingering near his lips after each bite. "Would you like a drink, Master?" she asked after he'd polished off the last of the shrimp, some cherry tomatoes and bite-size pieces of spicy beef-and-bean burritos.

"Just water." Just as he'd never drunk alcohol before playing football, he didn't indulge in drinking before or during sex games. "I don't want anything to interfere with my self-control or dull the delicious sensations I'm looking forward to enjoying with you." He paused, visually sampled her as well as the fruit still on the tray. "Those strawberries look mighty good. Bite into one and feed it to me."

Fully obedient, she lowered her head. His cock tightened against the zipper of his jeans when he watched her gleaming white teeth disappearing into the stem end of a berry. Then she raised her head and brought the fruit to his lips.

He bit into the sweet, juicy berry, swallowed. He licked away the juice from her mouth and his. It tasted tart, sweet, the way he imagined she'd be. "Where do you suggest we play this scene?" He didn't see a bed or a roomy sofa, doubted she'd like being fucked on the threadbare carpet any more than he would.

"My bedroom?" Her mouth curved in a smile. Not an ounce of nervousness, no protests that he was going too fast—but then this was the woman Dave had called a female predator. Colin got the feeling that while Susan might have fucked practically every unattached adult male in Hedgecock, she hadn't found what it took to satisfy her.

Besides, he wasn't auditioning her for sainthood, and she seemed just the sort of submissive lover he needed on his first night back in the town where his career had begun so long ago. A woman like Susan, who silently reminded him in no uncertain terms that while it might have been thirty-plus years since he'd left Hedgecock and while he might be fifty years old on his next birthday, he wasn't anywhere near dead. "That will work, unless there's a club around here where you'd rather play."

"There aren't any clubs in Hedgecock. Closest one I know of's in San Antonio. But I think you'll approve of my bedroom. It's sort of a playroom, Sir."

He raised an eyebrow. "Complete with toys?"

"Depends on what you mean by toys. There aren't any racks or St. Andrew's Crosses, if that's what you mean. But a single woman has to have her toys." She looked up at him, her lips curled into a seductive smile.

"You've got a pretty mouth. I want to feel it around my cock. Later," he added when she lowered her head as if to obey him *now*. "You said when we talked on the phone that you had details to go over tonight about the reunion events. Maybe we ought to get that over with first."

"All right." Rising gracefully, she crossed to a large folding table on the other side of the room. "Come here. As they say, a picture—in this case a program—is worth a thousand words."

He came up behind her, laid his hands on her shoulders and looked down at a recently done photo of himself on the cover of a glossy, four-color souvenir program for the reunion. "Where are the other guys?"

"Inside the program. As Hedgecock's first quarterback to make the pros, you get top billing." She flipped the program over to the back cover, where a montage of action shots showed him throwing, handing off, under center, celebrating after a touchdown pass in some long-ago game. "Your team had patriotic colors—red, white and blue. That's another reason I decided you had to be my cover guy."

"Yeah." She showed him the two-page inside spreads of Dave, Keith and Bobby. "You've done a nice job putting this program together."

"Thanks. You can have this one. The first event's on Wednesday, kicking off the football camp. Your Rebels have shown up in force to help out. We appreciate it even though most of them probably came for Dave's wedding and decided to stick around for the camp."

He was glad some members of his team had shown up for Dave's wedding on Saturday, and that they seemed ready to kick back and have some fun while acting as counselors at the camp. Colin wished he could have come early instead of checking out potential players at some universities ahead of next month's NFL draft. "I'm glad so many of them came. You and the rest of the committee have done a hell of a job, planning this reunion. I hope the school district will clear enough profits to repair the field and bleachers. It's obvious everyone in town has worked hard to make the event a success."

"Yes. We're all proud of our quarterbacks. You guys are the only things that make Hedgecock stand out from a hundred other tiny west Texas towns."

Colin set the program down. Looking at action photos taken of himself thirteen or more years ago made him feel ancient—older than he felt when he looked at the photo spreads of the other signal callers, all of whom were significantly younger than he. Hell, Bobby Anthony was young enough to be his son. Keith, too, although that would be a stretch. Only Dave belonged almost to his generation. "Turn around and hug me. Make me feel a little less decrepit."

As though she knew he needed an ego boost, Susan turned into his arms, her breath warm and sweet against his chest when she whispered, "You're not old. Just experienced. I like men who know what they're doing."

He bent, buried his face in the fragrant silk of her hair. "How do you know I know what I'm doing?"

"Instinct. There's just something about the way you look at me…the sound of your voice…"

He wanted to scoop her up, drag her to this bedroom she'd spoken about, devour her the way he hadn't done to a lover for years. Since Elise had walked out and gone home to New York less than a month after they'd moved, vowing she'd never set foot in Savannah again. "Go get that candle and the rose. Then turn the up volume on the music and show me the room where you want to play."

As he watched the fluid motion of that soft purple material against her thighs, her nicely rounded ass cheeks, the familiar heat of arousal curled around his belly, settled in his groin. Something about Susan made him feel powerful, strong—stronger than he'd felt since his playing years.

She handed him the candle then the rose. "If you'll follow me, I'll take you to my room." She paused, lowered her gaze. "Your room, Master."

"Ours." He hoped she wasn't one of those subs who got off on being called a slut or being punished for imagined misdeeds. "I'm into control, but I'm not into humiliation, just so you know."

"Thank you, Master." When he followed her into a small, sparsely furnished bedroom he closed the door then set the candle and rose on the single nightstand. He stepped back so he could watch the expression on her face as he unbuckled his belt and toed off his shoes.

"Strip for me." That low, sensual music filtered through the closed door, a sound that put him in mind of a private dungeon room, a fucking swing swaying to its beat. A woman—Susan—restrained in it while he stood watching her expressive face, fucking her slow and deep until she begged him to let her come. When she lifted that purple dress over her head and stood before him naked, head bowed, he wished that imaginary swing would materialize so he could take her on the sexual journey he'd just envisioned.

A faded pink rosebud tattooed on her smooth, hairless mound drew his gaze to her swollen clit. "Who put that there?"

"My first Master—my husband—had it done. He's been dead more than two years now." She opened the nightstand drawer, revealed some toys and a handful of wrapped condoms. "I like to come in here and play with my toys."

Colin glanced at the contents of the drawer then looked back at her gorgeous body, her full breasts, the large glittering stone in her navel. His gaze settled once more on the tattoo. Ordinarily he wasn't a fan of body art, but looking at hers made his sex rise painfully against his fly. He unzipped his jeans and drew it out, heard her gasp at first sight of his naked cock. The thick silver ring dangling from his Prince Albert piercing had a way of drawing that first response from lovers.

"Lie down on the bed. Pretend I've got you tied to the head and footboards. Don't say anything and don't move unless I tell you to."

Her cheeks flushed and her breathing quickened as she lay down and stretched both arms over her head. "Clasp your hands together." When she did, her breasts jutted out and he noticed the curved barbells in piercings just behind each nipple, imagined attaching a chain between them and tugging on it until she squirmed.

"Now your legs. Spread them as wide as you can. Make believe I'm going to tie one to each bedpost." Then he noticed the array of purple silk scarves she'd looped around the gleaming brass footboard. "Only it's not make-believe, is it?" Quickly he secured a scarf to either side of the bed frame at the level of her luscious hips.

Because he'd told her not to speak she shook her head. His big hands were surprisingly gentle as he picked up one foot, caressed it then positioned it next to her hip and tied it with a knot that let her know this wasn't the first time he'd bound a sub. He repeated the action with her other foot then stood back, giving her a good look at his huge, circumcised cock with that thick, silver ring threaded through its glistening eye. Its weight did nothing to pull down his rigid flesh that stood straight up against his washboard abs. When she thought of him ramming that monster tool in her cunt…her mouth…even up her ass, her mouth went dry.

"Spread your legs. I want to see if you're wet for me." When she bent her knees until they touched the cool, clean sheet he paused, ran his fingers over her swollen sex then brought them to his lips. "Oh, yeah. You're hot already. I can smell your arousal from here." His gaze settled between her legs, but he reached into the nightstand drawer and fumbled for the toy he wanted. She had to bite her tongue to keep from moaning out loud when he used her cunt to lube the butt plug then worked it slowly, tantalizingly, up her ass. Before she could think, he slid her dong-shaped vibrator into her wet, throbbing cunt and turned it on.

"God but you make me hot." He moved, more scarves in his hand. "I'm gonna blindfold you so you'll concentrate on the sensations and sounds." Eager to follow his order, she raised her head so he could tie a folded scarf over her eyes. Expecting him to tie her hands as well, she held them as high as she could above her head, but he only traced the shape of her lips with a finger. "I want your luscious mouth on my cock. Now."

Facing toward her vibrating cunt, he straddled her face, surrounding her with the heady smell of aroused male as he fed her his long, thick sex inch by inch until she was swallowing convulsively around the rigid flesh and the even harder ring embedded in its tip. Sensations rushed through her, a gagging sensation that brought more pleasure than pain, the tickling of his neatly trimmed pubic hair on her nose, her lips. When he tugged at her nipples and rotated the barbells with his fingers, sharp sensations invaded her, spread along highly sensitized nerve endings to her cunt, her ass.

She wanted to come but she didn't dare. Not until he gave her permission. Sucking harder, swallowing, she tried to concentrate on the heat and tickling sensation of his muscular thighs against her ears and face, the accelerating cadence of his breathing. But she couldn't ignore the vibrations in her cunt, or the sense of stretching and almost unbearable fullness in her ass. He reached for the nightstand again, she guessed from the shifting motion of the bed.

"Something tells me you like wax play. Much as I'd like to pleasure you that way, I won't do it without taking proper precautions and I don't see a way to do that here. For now you'll have to be satisfied with feeling me smooth warm wax onto you. I figure that if it's too hot for my fingers, it's too hot for your soft, precious skin. Your safe word is 'candle'." When he warned her, she gasped against his cock then sucked him harder

"Oh, yeah. Suck me." Susan held her breath, waiting for the sharp pain her Master had imprinted on her brain and wondering where the wax would fall. She anticipated the burning pain and delicious pleasure she hadn't experienced since Donnie used to coat her intimate flesh in molten wax. God but that had given her the most intense pleasure-pain she'd ever experienced.

But the wax wasn't terribly hot when Colin placed some on the tip of her nipple. The way he did it, though, the tiny sting sent needles of sensation almost as intense as if he'd dropped hot, melted wax directly onto her most sensitive flesh. She tightened her lips around his cock to keep from screaming at the intense feelings, feelings as much emotional as physical.

She kept sucking his cock, exploring the rigid, smooth flesh with her tongue as she braced herself for the wax to heat her other nipple, but it didn't. Instead he molded a palm full of the cooling wax around that same nipple, his touch soothing yet incredibly arousing. "Like that, do you?"

She couldn't answer. Didn't have to. The next sensation she had was of that wax in his hot palm landing on her clit and along her inner labia to where the vibrator base stopped it. Omigod! It hurt, not so much a living, breathing pain as one remembered from the past, triggered by the diluted sensation of slick, oily heat molding itself to her swollen clit, heightening the arousal. It hurt so damn good. Especially his long, agile fingers, smoothing and massaging the cooling wax against her clit, her mound.

"Babe, I've got to fuck you now." He sounded as though he were the one being tortured as he pulled out of her mouth and shifted on the bed. He was breathing hard by the time he withdrew the vibrator and reached in the drawer again. "I'm putting on a condom."

He knelt between her legs and removed the butt plug. When he sank into her cunt for the first time, she almost came. He was so...so big, so hot, so fucking alive. Yet gentle. Almost as if she were a virgin, he fucked her slowly, a little at a time until she felt his balls bouncing against her cunt lips. God but he stretched her until it hurt—a delicious hurt that had every cell in her body screaming for release. She shifted as much as she could, trying to take him deeper, seeking the climax that hung just outside her reach.

Because he hadn't told her she could come, she clamped down on her own lips. If she hadn't, she'd have begged him for release. Then she felt him shudder, felt his hot cock shuddering in her cunt.

"Come, baby. Come for me now or it will be too late."

She let go as he took her lips, captured her screams in his mouth. His body shook when he sank hard into her and came in hot, staccato bursts of semen she felt against the mouth of her womb, even through the latex barrier.

After what could have been a minute or an hour—she didn't know—he withdrew. But he didn't release her bonds. Instead he lay between her legs, his mouth on her flesh, licking and nipping at her pussy lips, her mound, her tingling wax-covered clit until he closed his mouth over her cunt and tongue-fucked her until she was ready to come again.

Then he peeled off the wax, ever so gently. "Tell me about this." He traced the rose tattoo with one finger. Though he spoke softly, it was nonetheless a demand.

Her voice felt as if she hadn't spoken in years, as though Colin's cock had left a permanent impression on her throat. "It was a wedding present, twenty-one years ago. My Master had it done after he shaved my pussy the first time. Said he didn't like hair there, but he didn't want me looking plain."

Colin turned his head, tongued the flower above her clit. "I like it. I don't like that somebody else had it done to you. Tell me about him."

"He claimed me as his slave when I was just eighteen. He was fifty-two at the time. But he gave me what no vanilla lover ever had—the feeling of being his property, of being loved and cared for. Of being safe. He taught me to like the kink. To expect it, but most of all to want to give him back all the pleasure he gave me." In the dark, blindfolded, she could almost imagine Donnie was back, until she felt Colin's hard-muscled body, his massive sex, which didn't need a lot of encouragement to get it up and going. "I loved him. When he died two years ago, I wished I could have gone with him."

"Did he have your nipples and navel pierced, too?"

"No." She reached down, sank her fingers into his hair. "I had the piercings done when I was in high school, as I'm sure Dave Delaney and all the other boys at school can attest to. Until Donnie took me and gave me what I needed, I developed a well-deserved reputation as a slut. Some folks say I've become one again since he died."

"So you haven't found another Dom?" His warm breath tickled her clit, made it long for his mouth.

"Not until now." Susan stroked Colin's head, liked the feel of his crisp, short hair beneath her fingers. "Donnie was bald. Had just a little ring of hair around here. He used to make me shave his head every day. Thought he looked better completely bald."

Colin fingered her cunt, his touch teasing. "I haven't shaved my head for years, since my ex-wife wanted me to do it for a club scene back in New York. I figure, since my ancestors provided me a full head of hair, I probably ought to keep it. Maybe I'll shave it all off when I turn completely gray."

"I like your hair the way it is. There's always hair dye if you don't like gray hair. I've never done much club play, so nobody's ever given me the impression that all Doms have to wear black leather and shave their heads."

"Good. I'm not much into black leather, although I've got a mask, a pair of chaps and a Gates of Hell that I sometimes put on for club scenes. I am a Dom, though. I've always thought that involved more what's inside my head than the trappings some Doms adopt to define themselves. Take off the blindfold now and toss me a couple of those pillows. This time I want you to see who's claiming you." When he sat back on his heels, she met his hot, passionate gaze as she handed him the pillows. "Damn it, you're the most gorgeous submissive I've ever had."

Susan had seen pictures of Elise Zanardi, Colin's beautiful former wife and daughter of one of the owners of the team he'd played for. She'd looked them up on the internet after learning Colin would be coming back to Hedgecock for the reunion. "I doubt that, Master. But thank you anyhow." When he slapped her thigh lightly, she raised her hips so he could position the pillows beneath her butt.

He traced around her rear hole with his finger, frowned. "Where's the bathroom?"

"First door to your left. Would you like me to help?" She wanted to kneel at his feet and taste his semen, cleanse his massive cock with her mouth then with a warm, wet washcloth.

His smile could have lit up a football field. "Nope. Just stay here. Think about how your ass will feel, stuffed with my cock. It isn't your ass, though, it's mine. I own your mouth and your cunt, and I intend to own this, too." He stroked around her rim once more than got up and left.

* * * * *

Colin got rid of the condom and rinsed off. Then he got naked, wanting to feel the sub he'd just claimed, skin to skin. He glanced in the mirror, a critical look that reassured him his taut, conditioned body hadn't suddenly gone to hell since he'd showered and shaved at the hotel in Midland that morning. Then the smooth ring dangling from his cock caught his eye. He'd had the piercing since college, more specifically since a drunken fraternity road trip that had included a group visit to a Dallas piercing and tattoo parlor. Over the years he'd fucked women's asses, even Elise's, with the ring in place. But Susan had felt damn tight when he'd inserted that butt plug. The ring might savage her tender tissue. Sitting on the closed toilet seat, he released the captive bead and worked the metal around and out. For some reason the familiar act reminded him how he used to remove the ring when he dressed before every game.

He'd done that to prevent injury to himself. Now he wanted to keep from hurting Susan. He'd get her to put it back in. Later. Standing and setting it on the vanity, he made his way back to the playroom. And his new, beautifully submissive lover.

She hadn't moved a muscle. His gaze settled on her glistening slit, her tempting rear hole now fully accessible. For the first time he noticed that the slender stem of her rose tattoo wound around her clit and seemed to disappear inside her slick, wet cunt. His balls tightened, and his cock reared straight up against his belly.

Fuck, it was crazy, the way she made him rock-hard without him touching her—even after he'd come in her less than a half-hour ago. He moved to the side of the bed, bent, claimed her mouth and tasted it with his tongue. Her breathing was ragged, her pulse rapid, as though she knew what was coming and wanted it, the pain and the pleasure.

"I took the ring out of my cock." He whispered it near her lips, watched her eyes tear up. Relief? Disappointment? "Didn't want to risk hurting you. You can put it back in. Later."

She nodded, laid one hand on his upper arm.

"You may talk if you want to, baby." He wanted to hear her voice, needed her to tell him what was going through her pretty head. "Wanna see?"

"I'd be honored to taste." She smiled up at him then glanced around his arm at his erection. "You're one gorgeous man, and not just your big, beautiful cock. Any woman would be proud to call you Master."

"Keep that in mind for later." Colin wasn't ready to put the thought in words just yet, but he was already thinking he didn't mean the claiming to be for just while he was here. He let himself imagine taking her back to Savannah, dominating her in every way a man could dominate one woman, going to sleep with her and waking up to find her mouth on his morning erection, servicing him with a smile. Taking her to play at the club, indulging her fetish for wax play while restraining her on the spiderweb, the fucking swing...

Strangely, he didn't envision sharing her though he'd gotten off on threesomes for the nearly twenty years he'd been married to Elise. Maybe that would change later, when the new wore off. Now he wanted all of Susan. Her mouth, her cunt...her tight little ass. He kissed her again, tongue-fucking her luscious mouth as he enjoyed the way her small hands dug into his shoulders and her hot, wet pussy cradled his hard-on. When he finally broke the kiss he took a couple of condoms and some lubricant from the drawer.

Seeing a cock-shaped gag toward the back of the drawer, he took it out, too. "Open your mouth for me."

Perfectly compliant, she did, and he inserted the gag, securing it with elastic bands that went around her head. "Your safe word won't do much good right now. Jerk on my hair if I hurt you too much. I want your pleasure, and I only want to inflict the degree of pain it takes to make it good for you."

Then he bent and kissed her clit before reinserting her vibrator and setting it in motion. "Sexy baby, aren't you?" Kneeling then sliding his knees to the sides of the pillows under her butt cheeks, he rolled on a condom then opened the lubricant and smeared it over himself. For good measure he worked two heavily lubricated fingers up her ass.

For a minute he petted her clit, traced around the vibrator and along her wet, slick slit to her tight little asshole. It glistened, beckoned him. Another time he'd rim her with his tongue but now he needed to get inside her. He removed his fingers, wiped away the excess lube and carefully positioned his cock. Then he pressed forward. God but she was so tight it hurt him when he penetrated her anal sphincter.

When he looked up at her, tears flowed from her eyes and she moaned softly around the gag. But she didn't pull his hair or try to talk around the gag. Her flesh slowly relaxed around him, let him move deeper. She felt like heaven and hell. The vibrator in her cunt sent its sensations through the thin wall of tissue that separated the two chambers, made him desperate to come.

The tone of her moaning changed. Her inner muscles gripped him in a rhythmic motion and she started raising her hips to meet his thrusts. Her nipples stood firm and pebbled in front of the gleaming barbells, beckoning his hands. He cupped her full breasts, caught both her nipples between his thumbs and forefingers. Squeezed hard when the tight muscles in her ass clamped down on his cock. "Yeah, baby, fuck me like this."

He'd already come once tonight and he was nearly fifty years old. He should be wrung out and hung to dry, but damn if she didn't make him feel as sexually powerful as he'd been twenty years ago. Wanting to slow down, enjoy the incredible sensations, he bent and licked the tops of her breasts, her throat. Pulling on her nipples, he brought them to his lips and sucked them, liking the alien feel of the jewelry against his lips and tongue.

Her hands tightened on his shoulders, caressing him, using him for leverage while she lifted her hips higher, harder until his balls were bouncing against her butt.

He couldn't take any more. "Stop!"

Though she lay beneath him trembling, she obeyed his order but she shot him a questioning look.

"Take out the vibrator. Now."

While she did, he pulled out of her rear hole, changed condoms and released the scarves from her legs. Jerking the pillow out from under her, he slid into her cunt. "My cunt is where I want to come. Wrap these gorgeous legs around my waist."

The slapping sounds of his balls against her ass surrounded them. Looking at her beautiful mouth stretched around the gag and her glistening nipples red from his attention almost made him come, but it was the feel of her practiced vaginal muscles caressing his cock and the heady smells and tastes of him and her and sex on his tongue that made him think of collars. Long-term ties he'd vowed never to consider again after Elise.

"My beautiful slave," he murmured when he watched her come, her muffled moans setting off his own climax.

He'd never before thought he might want children, but he wished as he came in the rubber that he could make her pregnant before it was too late for both of them. A damn crazy thought, for certain, but it lingered in the back of his mind as she lay curled in his arms.

Chapter Two

છ

When they got up to shower later, Colin draped his arm around Susan's waist. Though the distance from the bed to the bathroom wasn't more than twenty feet, he stopped twice to lift her chin and take her mouth. Not ravenous kisses but ones that seemed to convey tenderness, a sort of caring that went beyond sexual satisfaction. He turned on the water and adjusted the temperature before holding out his hand and bringing her beside him under the soft, warm spray.

He took the shampoo, lathered her hair then rinsed the sweet-smelling foam away. "You please me more than I'd dreamed might be possible at this point in my life." His admission sounded raw, as though it came straight from his heart.

Dared she hope for more than this wonderful week with a sexual Dominant who could bring her to submission and blissful pleasure, not to mention the hottest man who'd ever fucked her? Colin had to be her wildest fantasy come true. "You please me, too, Master." She'd have said more, told him how she'd love to be his full-time slave—24/7 if that was what he needed.

But he scared her, not by what he demanded, but by who he was. Unlike Donnie, he was rich and powerful, former all-pro quarterback and now head coach of the Savannah Rebels. On top of that, he had a face and body guaranteed to attract every woman with eyes and active hormones. Colin could have any woman he wanted, any time or place.

She was Hedgecock's teenage slut who'd grown up and stayed in town, spent twenty years with one Master. Worse, she'd sampled way more than her share of men while seeking the elusive pleasure she'd hadn't found since Donnie's death. Until tonight.

Colin bent and lifted her wet hair, kissed the back of her neck. "What's the matter, baby?"

He had to have heard about her reputation. She recalled hitting on Dave Delaney at Keith and Tina's wedding, figured Dave had probably told Colin. If he hadn't, there were a few local assholes who'd tried to hit on her and didn't mind calling her all sorts of names because she'd told the disgusting creatures no. "Since my Master died I've fucked a lot of men. I was looking for…"

Colin reached around her, brought her closer until they stood, spoon fashion, her back flush against his hard-muscled chest. Water cascaded over them. "You were looking for me. As long as we're together you won't need to look any farther to find satisfaction. Understand?"

"Yes. I'm yours. Only yours, as long as you want me." If he'd been Donnie, she'd have gone to her knees, kissed his feet, hoped he'd force her head down onto his cock, use his favorite flogger on her back. But Colin wasn't her old Master. And Susan had the feeling he expected only her simple assurance that she was his. His and no one else's unless he chose to share her.

"Good. Let's dry off and go back to bed." He shut off the water and dried them then handed her the thick, smooth, surprisingly lightweight piece of jewelry he'd taken out of his beautiful cock. "I'll let you put that back in now."

* * * * *

The next morning Colin woke first and looked at Susan. Her dark, silky hair tickled his arm, reminding him she was very real and not an incredibly arousing dream. She shifted toward him and laid her hand gently on his thigh. Her small hand looked pale against his deeply tanned skin.

He'd claimed her as his submissive. But he wanted more.

Full-time enslavement? It was too soon. Still he felt as strongly now that he wanted Susan as he had years ago when he'd first seen Elise at a team party, all glitter and pale gold from the top of her gleaming head to the hem of the skin-tight sheath gown that had brushed her ankles. A trophy, only not for the glass case in his game room but for his bed.

He'd had to claim Elise back then. He felt the same way about Susan now.

Not that Susan was a team owner's daughter, or that by claiming her he'd earn the respect and admiration of the team or his fellow coaches. Certainly not in a town where she admitted she'd sought but not found the man who could fill a gaping void in her life. But Colin had the feeling he'd find something more in her sweet, submissive arms. Satisfaction, not just the sexual kind, but something more. He sensed he could come home to her every night and feel the same way every day for the rest of his life.

She shifted, came closer as though to absorb his body heat. "Good morning, little one," he said, nuzzling her hair and laying a hand on her thigh. "Let's go have breakfast at the café. I want to show you off, make my guys jealous."

"All right." He lay back against the pillows and watched her scurry around the room. She hesitated then chose a long khaki skirt and tailored shirt from the closet. From a dresser drawer she fished out a lacy pink bra and matching bikini panties.

Good. He didn't want her sashaying around town with a bare ass, even if he'd be the only one who'd know she was naked beneath the casual, inexpensive outfit. And he approved her choice of the long skirt because he didn't want her giving his players the pleasure of ogling her gorgeous legs.

"I'd better go grab some clean clothes, too." The jeans and shirt he'd worn yesterday probably looked as though he'd slept in them, or tossed them heedlessly to a wet bathroom floor, which he'd done in his hurry to get back to Susan.

* * * * *

She loved the way Colin held her hand when they walked into the café and later, while they moseyed down the dusty main street to the school so she could check out arrangements with Melanie Tate and the other local people who were helping with final preparations for the festivities.

"So how did you manage to get all this done?" Colin sounded impressed.

"Teamwork. Same way I imagine you got your team all the way to the Super Bowl last season. We — that is, everybody in Hedgecock — know that we have to make this reunion a success to raise money. If we don't, the bleachers and athletic fields will fall apart any day now and somebody will get hurt."

He glanced over toward the fields, grinned. "You know, until you asked me to come to this reunion, I hadn't thought about Hedgecock for years. Being here again brings back memories that must have been buried in the back of my mind."

"Good ones, I hope."

He grinned but she noticed a faraway look in his deep brown eyes. "Mostly. It gives a kid a rush, having everybody think he's good at a sport, particularly at a position that's as visible as quarterback. Because I'd had to leave San Antonio and move in with my dad after Mom got killed, the high I got from being the hometown football hero here was probably less pronounced than it would have been if I'd lived here all my life, grown up playing with my teammates. Not to mention that Dad wasn't one to lay roots anywhere. I knew that when his work was done, we'd be moving on, so Hedgecock was just a stopping point for me. I never let it feel like home."

"Like Dave and the others did?" Though Susan had put together brief bios about all the quarterbacks' high school careers, her interest almost from the first had been for Colin. Not because he'd been the first of the four to play in the NFL, but because his handsome face had captivated her from the first glimpse she'd had of his photo. He was even better in person than he'd been in her late-night fantasies.

"I guess." He headed toward the field, practically dragging her along with him as she struggled to match his long, decisive stride. Next to the rusty bleachers now, he stopped in his tracks. "Jesus. These bleachers are disasters waiting to happen. I had no idea they were this bad."

"Time tends to do a number on metal, especially when it's outside in the sun and rain. According to the research Mel did into old school records, these bleachers were built years before you were born. By the way, Mel is Bobby's mom. She and Cal Tate got married last fall. All of us, and Dave, went to high school around the same time."

As though mesmerized, Colin stepped away, toward the field where he'd started his long, storied career. "Coach Williams taught me how to throw out here. I set up a similar arrangement to that for my quarterbacks to use in Savannah to improve their accuracy," he said, gesturing toward the series of barrel staves hung sideways on ropes suspended from the goalposts. "Of course I had the staves fabricated from stainless steel and hung from posts on one end of a practice field. I have trouble imagining the school district not having taken better care of the facilities over the years."

"Hedgecock has had hard times. The oil fields have pretty much played out. Droughts have taken a toll on the cattle industry. A lot of folks have moved away over the past few years." She paused then met Colin's gaze. "Cal's family has owned the bank here for generations, and he kept digging into his pockets as long as he could. He's the one who came up with the idea for a reunion."

"I had no idea things were that bad."

"You'd have had no reason to know."

Colin shook his head. "I'm glad you persuaded me to come back. With a little luck, the football camp and reunion activities will bring in a bundle."

"We're keeping our fingers crossed." Susan thought about the throwing competition Cal had set up for Saturday, along with some other football-related activities to amuse attendees and hopefully separate them from their money. "I bet you've been out there on the field in Savannah, practicing for the competition coming up on Saturday."

"You're right. It surprised the hell out of me, finding out I can still throw a football seventy yards, given a brisk tailwind and a lot of luck." He turned to her, grinned. In workout shorts and a Rebels jersey that showed off his muscular legs and arms, he looked as if he could go out on that field and get back into the game if he wanted to. "I'm not the sort of guy who'd let himself get shown up too badly by the younger guys. Did you think I would be?"

"No, Master." She said it quietly, in case the bleachers had ears. "The consensus around here is that Bobby Anthony will win the throwing competition, though. Guess it's because folks remember him best."

"It's because Bobby's the biggest and youngest of us, and he's got the strongest arm. He won't win, though, because he throws a little bit wild. Not that he won't improve with practice—he's damn good for a rookie. He's got a great career ahead of him if he manages to stay healthy down in Orlando." Colin paused, frowned. "Right now Keith is more accurate and has almost as strong an arm. Dave is, too, only he's going to be hampered by that injury to his knee."

"I'm putting my bet on you."

He laughed and drew her up close to his side. "As my perfect little sub should. Seriously, Keith would be the best bet to win. Unless…"

Colin had a wistful look on his handsome face when he looked at the barrel staves.

"Why'd you retire when you did?" He'd only been thirty-seven, and as far as she knew he hadn't suffered a career-ending injury the way Dave had in the last Super Bowl.

"I wanted to go out on top, not hang on until my father-in-law and my teammates started praying I'd retire. I'm glad I did, because I don't suffer constant pain the way a lot of former players do." He paused. "I was lucky never to get any serious injuries. Even luckier that I had the best offensive line in the game protecting my ass. I still send presents to those guys every Christmas."

"And well you should, since they took care of you so well. It thrills me to know you're still in one very hot piece. Master."

He drew her into his arms, bent and kissed her. "Want to go play under the bleachers?"

"You've got to be kidding. There's an inch-thick layer of rust you're asking me to get embedded in my backside. Not to mention it's broad daylight."

"I'd let you lay your pretty butt on my letter jacket. If I still had it, that is." His teasing tone let her know he wasn't serious.

"Okay." She looked up at him. "Uh-oh. Here come Dave and Diane. They've got his dog with them."

"She looks like Keith." Colin made no move to let Susan step out of his loose embrace.

"Daisy?"

He laughed. "No, silly. Diane."

"Don't you mean Keith looks like her? She's older."

"She looks well enough preserved to me, but she's nowhere near as gorgeous as you." Colin nuzzled her neck. "Weren't you two pals when you were kids?" he asked.

"Diane hated me, just like all the other girls who thought I was a slut. Most likely she still does, especially since I tried to hit on Dave at Keith and Tina's wedding." Susan couldn't help the twinge of regret that admission cost her. "You might not want to be seen cozying up to me."

"I couldn't care less what anybody might think. I'm with the hottest woman in Hedgecock and I want everybody to know it. Come here." When he ordered it, she had no choice but to tilt her head, wrap her arms around her Master's muscular neck and surrender to his deep, passionate kiss.

"Hey, coach, take it to your bedroom," Dave said as he and Diane came up and joined them. "Want to get in a little practice?"

Colin shot a dubious look at Dave. "Don't tell me you think you're in any shape for throwing. Hadn't you better take your bride home and play with her?"

"Soon enough, pal. Seriously, I don't want to make a fool of myself out there on Saturday. Come on, let's toss a few balls, work the kinks out. Daisy, you stay here and keep the girls company." The sooty poodle sat on her haunches, an expectant look on her face.

Dave reached in his pocket and fished out a treat for her and was rewarded with a wiggle and a "woof".

"She still minds you," Colin said, shaking his head. "Never thought I'd let a dog on the practice field until you showed me she's fully under your control."

"Gotta control somebody. It's for sure I don't have your talent for controlling my women. Let's go see if we can still throw."

When the two went out on the field, Colin towing the wheeled box full of footballs Diane had been pulling behind her, Susan and Diane stood staring at one another. An uneasy silence settled between them. Finally Susan couldn't stand it any longer. "Congratulations on your marriage."

Diane managed a stiff smile. "Thank you."

This wasn't going to be easy. Maybe it was best that they just watched the guys. Turning toward the field, Susan saw Dave and Colin throwing a ball back and forth. With each throw Colin moved farther back. "Both of them look good," Susan commented, to break the silence.

"Yes. They do. I know the competition on Saturday's just for fun, but I don't think Dave has it in him to go out and not try his best to win." Diane frowned. "I remember seeing Colin play here when I was little. Dad used to take me to all his games. It looks as though he's as determined as Dave not to let Keith and Bobby show him up too badly."

"He told me he's been practicing ever since he agreed to take part in the competition." To Susan, it seemed Colin had the edge on Dave, but she knew she was prejudiced. "Dave looks good, too, but then he hasn't been retired for twelve or thirteen years."

An uncomfortable silence settled over them again, and for a long time they focused their attention on what the guys were doing.

Susan couldn't stand it any longer. "Look, Diane, I know how you must feel toward me. I wish we could be friends. I'm damn sorry I made a play for Dave at your brother's wedding."

Diane turned, met her gaze. "I'd still be mad if I weren't so happy. I just wish this reunion weren't delaying our honeymoon." She paused, as if she was trying to decide whether to say more. "It looks like you've latched on to Colin. Don't hurt him the way you have so many men since your husband died." As though she'd said all she intended to say, she bent and scratched Daisy's curly topknot.

"I won't." The only person who'd be hurt was Susan herself, when Colin decided he didn't want her anymore. "Look, Diane. There are qualities I need in a man, things you wouldn't understand. I haven't found them since Donnie died—until now."

Diane shrugged. "Looks as though the guys are about to have some company."

Keith and Bobby were crossing the field with their wives. Keith was riding his son on his shoulders then laughingly set the toddler down next to Tina. When the men veered off toward the field, Tina and Marly followed little Jack as he toddled toward the bleachers. "That's right, go to Aunt Diane," Tina told the little guy when he made a beeline for Diane and latched on to her jeans-clad leg.

The kid was precious, with blond hair, blue eyes and a huge smile. Susan watched him play, wondered...

Since he'd already had grown children he hardly ever saw by the time he'd married Susan, Donnie hadn't wanted any more kids. She hadn't minded, or at least she'd never admitted it even to herself. Now, though, she wondered. Must be her biological clock ticking, reminding her of the fact she'd be forty in three more months. Colin and his ex-wife hadn't had children, either, she'd learned from reading about him on the internet. Would he want—

Don't even think about it, idiot. But Susan couldn't help dreaming, imagining them not only as Master and slave but as a family. When Bobby's wife Marly said something about her and Bobby deciding to wait awhile before having kids, Susan wished she had the luxury of time.

When she glanced out at the guys, she noticed they'd moved close to the four corners of the field and were throwing in earnest, not just lobbing the ball around. Colin caught a laser shot from Bobby then launched a perfect spiral to Keith. "They'd better be careful out there."

"Nobody's wearing gloves," Marly observed. "If they don't take it easy, somebody's gonna end up with a broken finger."

"Oh, my, I hope not. Jack, no!" Tina ran to the bleachers, lifted the toddler off the rusty bottom row then nuzzled his chubby cheek as she rejoined the other women. Setting him down next to her, she said, "Now you stay right here, sweetie."

Marly, apparently the most fanatical football fan of the four, kept her eyes glued on the men. "That's amazing."

Diane shot her an amused grin. "What's so amazing?"

"Coach Zanardi hasn't played for years but he can still throw almost as hard as Bobby."

Diane smiled. "Dave says it's not the arms that usually go, it's their legs that make them give up playing. I wonder who'll win the competition."

"Colin told me he'd bet on Keith," Susan said. "But it looks to me like they're pretty even."

Marly watched a minute then turned back to the others. "Bobby throws the hardest."

Not wanting to burst the hot little cheerleader's bubble, Susan didn't pass along what Colin had said about Bobby's uncertain accuracy. "They're just playing around. We'll have to wait 'til Saturday to see who's going to win the competition."

She wished Cal Tate, who'd organized the sports part of the reunion events, would have agreed to go out there and try his own hand at the passing contest. After all, he'd been a Hedgecock County High School quarterback right after Dave, and he'd earned a football scholarship, too.

"Is Cal going to throw with them?" Diane, who'd been a year ahead of Susan in school, voiced the same question Susan had asked Cal months earlier.

"No. Mel and I asked him when we were planning the competition, but he said he hadn't picked up a football since he got hurt in college, other than to play around with his sons. Pity. We might have had five Hedgecock quarterbacks go to the NFL."

"If Mr. Tate had gone pro, who would have run the bank? It's been in his family for years and years." Tina picked Jack up again when he started to fuss, rocked him against her body. "There, sweetie, I know it's past time for your nap."

About then the guys quit showing off. Or did they? Other than Dave, they all seemed to be racing for the closer of the two goalposts, Bobby in the lead. Colin wasn't more than a step behind. Crazy. That's what he was. Susan shook her head, figured she'd be spending the afternoon massaging the muscles Colin had probably strained in his determination to keep up.

Limping along at a leisurely pace, Dave brought up the rear. At least he hadn't gone insane. But then Susan had seen him using crutches as recently as last week. He probably had no business being out there at all, considering his recently repaired knee.

"I guess Keith didn't feel like pushing it." Marly grinned at Bobby when he joined them, and she did a little double take when Colin came up and took Susan in his arms.

"That's not it at all," Diane offered. "My little brother doesn't run unless a three-hundred-pound defensive end — or maybe a bull — is bearing down on him."

Keith kissed Tina then hoisted Jack high above his head. "I beat your brand-new husband, didn't I?" he asked Diane, and she made a funny face at him. "Bet I could get away from Bullyboy, too."

From what Susan had heard, the aging bull Diane's son kept as a pet wouldn't give anybody much of a fight, so she laughed when Dave protested that he wouldn't give the animal a shot at him.

They all seemed to enjoy the friendly banter, even Dave who took a ribbing for having tired himself out since his wedding two days earlier. Susan figured as they split up and walked away that when they were out on the field Saturday in front of what promised to be a huge crowd, they'd pull out all the stops.

* * * * *

Colin felt good. Damn good. He'd held his own, throwing with three pro quarterbacks who were decades younger. He'd even managed to beat everybody in a forty-yard sprint except for the twenty-three-year-old kid who had at least three inches of height on him. A warm west Texas wind ruffled Colin's hair, and he had his hand resting on the hip of a hot sexual submissive. His submissive.

"Where to now?" Susan laid her hand over his on her hip as they left the Burger Den that hadn't changed much since he'd eaten there some thirty years ago.

He liked the fact that she deferred to him, loved her soft, incredibly arousing drawl. "You're the one who lives here. What do you do for fun?"

Even her laugh sounded sexy. "Not a lot. Other than working on stuff for the reunion, or going back to my house and playing with my toys. But I imagine you're too tired for that."

"Don't count on it, baby." This woman could get his cock to stand up and take notice, better than anybody he'd run into for longer than he could remember. "I could use a sexy massage first, though."

"As in both of us stark naked, Master?"

"Oh, yeah. That's the best kind." A hell of a lot better than the massages he got at the training facility after he worked out. Colin considered the impersonal pummeling of sore muscles punctuated with mutterings by the Rebels' head trainer that he was too old to be throwing footballs and lifting weights, and that he ought to be out with the sensible retirees playing shuffleboard or a lazy game of par-three golf. "Let's go do it."

"Let's." She looked up at him, her eyes sparkling as though she thought he'd hung the moon.

He imagined her naked, straddling his ass while she worked the tightness out of his shoulders. And on her knees between his legs, kneading his thighs. Or... Fuck, he was getting hard as stone just thinking about what he'd have her do to him. "Afterward we'll make love, and then we'll curl up together like two hibernating bears and take a nap. Tonight I want to take you to that barbecue at the café. I can already smell ribs cooking, and it makes me hungry. Would you like that?"

"Yes, Master. I'd like that a lot." She looked up at him, smiled. What he really appreciated was that she didn't say a word about him needing rest or being too tired for sex.

He loved her for not reminding him his calf muscles were aching and his right shoulder and elbow were letting him know he'd given them a good workout. "I'm glad." Damn. Susan made him feel like she believed he could conquer the world, and that felt good. Real good.

* * * * *

Susan had never been a sports groupie, never understood some women's compulsion to chase after guys just because they were athletes. As she worked some icy menthol-scented massage gel Colin had fished out of his travel bag into his heavily muscled back and arms, she began to understand why those women fixated on jocks. There was something about Colin's hard, well-conditioned body that had her getting wet between her legs.

Of course she knew what this particular body could do to hers. But still...

"Rub a little harder, baby. I won't break."

She exerted more pressure with her hands and fingers, glad for once that her nails were short. "Feel good?"

He let out a low, rumbling sound—almost a purr. "Yeah. Feels real good. I could get used to feeling your hands on me like this."

She could get used to it, too. She loved touching him, feeling how the crisp texture of his body hair contrasted with his firm, smooth skin. He felt healthy beneath her hands. Full of life.

Had Donnie ever felt like this? She tried to remember the early times, before he'd gotten old and sick. No, even then Donnie had been paunchy, a bit overweight. He'd put away burgers and fries with gusto, and he'd loved his beer. But he'd taken care of her as no one ever had before. Susan had loved him until he'd drawn his last, wheezing breath while she'd held his hand in the other bedroom, the one she hadn't been able to sleep in since his death.

Colin seemed, from what little she'd seen, to eat a fairly healthy diet that hadn't so far included any beer at all. Considering the choices available for breakfast at the café and at the Burger Den where they'd grabbed a quick lunch. Yeah, he'd chowed down on bacon and eggs for breakfast and a fried chicken sandwich for lunch, minus the usual fries. He obviously had to fuel his big body with something, and there hadn't been healthier choices.

Moving down toward the end of the bed to work on his calves and thighs, she looked at him over his shoulder. "I can tell you take good care of your body. I'm sorry Hedgecock doesn't have any restaurants that serve healthy foods. I'd cook for you, but everything's so crazy, with getting ready for the reunion."

He laughed. "That's okay, baby. I'll manage for a few days. I may even lose a pound or two."

As far as she was concerned, he was absolutely perfect the way he was. "You look great. I bet you don't weigh an ounce over…" She tried to remember the other players' listed playing weights. "Two thirty."

"Two fifteen. The last few years I played, I weighed in around two twenty. I'm only a hair over six two, not six four or five like Keith and Bobby. I'm not especially big-boned, either. If I weighed two thirty, I'd look like the Pillsbury Dough Boy. I imagine I'd move like him, too. Ahhh, yeah. Dig into that left calf muscle, loosen it up."

She felt the tightness, massaged it with the fingers of both hands until she felt the tension ease. "Feel better now?"

"Much better. Come up here. There are some parts of you I want to massage."

Her pussy, she hoped. Just touching him, feeling him beneath her hands, had her soaking wet. Setting the tube of icy massage gel on the nightstand, Susan lay down on her side next to her Master and awaited his pleasure.

He drew her close, so close she heard his heart beating strong and slow, felt its steady cadence against her breasts. His calloused fingers reminded her of his toughness, his mastery, while his lazy exploration of the length of her back coaxed the sort of trust she'd never found easy to bestow on a lover.

He paused, his long fingers splayed over her butt. "Imagine someone's watching us, wondering if I'll slide my hand lower, rim your luscious asshole, or if I'll roll you over and claim your sopping cunt instead. If it's a man, he'll get hard. His breathing will grow ragged. Maybe he'll pull his dick out and jerk off, wishing he were me touching you. Claiming you for himself.

"But maybe it's a woman. She's getting hot and wet imagining she's you and that I'm rock-hard to fuck her needy little ass. You like that idea, don't you, pet?"

"Yes, Master." It might be perverse, but Susan imagined a lot of mean women who'd called her names watching while Colin pleasured her. She'd relish feeding their sexual neediness. "Any woman would be jealous, watching you pleasuring me. You're so hot—hotter than any man she's ever seen. Hotter than any I've ever seen, too."

"I'm glad you think so." With a sexy growl Colin rolled her onto her back, grabbed a condom from the drawer and rolled it down his throbbing erection. Then he spread her legs with his knees as he came down on top of her and buried his big cock all the way inside her until his ring tickled the tip of her womb and his testicles rested between her wet, swollen labia. "I kind of like thinking some men are watching and that they're all jealous as hell because your pretty cunt's all mine. It is, isn't it?"

"Yes. Oh God, your cock feels so good inside me. So huge and hard and…omigod!" With every stroke he stretched her more, his motion slow, delicious. How would it feel if he came now, if his hot, wet semen flooded her body without that condom in the way?

She clamped down on him with her inner muscles. If only she could hold him there, she'd never ask anything more.

"Oh yeah, squeeze me. I want you to come for me. Now." He bent, took her mouth, forced her lips apart and ravished her there while he fucked her harder, deeper. He looped his arms around her knees, changed the angle of penetration.

God yes. She'd tensed up, held back, but now he wanted her to come and she was glad to obey. When she came apart in his arms he took her screams of pleasure, swallowed them, reveled in the incredible thrill of climax.

Mine and his, she thought, holding him as he reached his own pleasure while his cock pulsated with life deep inside her body.

Chapter Three

ഇ

"I doubt the café has had this much business in years. Maybe ever." Susan leaned back in her chair early that evening, loving the warm, protective feel of Colin's hand resting on her shoulder. "Looks like everybody in town came here tonight to get some of the ribs."

Colin nodded across the room at Bobby and Marly who were sitting with Cal and Mel Tate. "No time to cook, with all that's going on, getting ready for the football camp—that would be my guess."

"Either that or everybody smelled these ribs cooking and opted to come have some. The food here may not be all that healthy but it tastes good. There come Dave and Keith with their wives and kids."

Dave stopped and spoke with the Rebels' players then joined the others.

"Looks like Hedgecock may be growing itself another quarterback," Colin commented. "Who's the big kid?"

"That's Dylan Granger. Diane's son. He's around fourteen—a ninth grader."

Colin sat for a minute, as though deep in thought. "Granger? I don't remember a lot of people from here, but that name rings a bell."

"Frank Granger?"

"Big guy, six four or five, close to three hundred pounds? The sonofabitch was a ninth grader when I was a senior. Had a smartass mouth on him, apparently thought he could take me on." Colin massaged the bridge of his nose, grimaced. "I showed him he was wrong, but he left me with a broken nose and a bunch of bruises. I hurt like hell for a week or so. Not just my body but my ego. After all, I was nearly eighteen and he was three or four years younger."

Susan looked closely at Colin's straight, slightly prominent nose and doubted Frank had done any lasting damage. Then she glanced over at Dave and Diane. "You've got something in common with Diane, then. Frank used to use her for a punching bag until she finally got smart and threw him out. He loved to fight, I guess, since he took up riding bulls in the rodeo."

"I hope for Frank's sake that he's got enough sense to stay away this week. If he comes back, it sounds as though there'll be guys lined up three deep, wanting to exact some revenge."

Susan smiled. "Old Frank's safely in hell. He's been dead for several years, thanks to a bull at a rodeo up in Denver."

"Good riddance." Colin dug into another slab of ribs, glanced over at the big table where the Rebels' players were eating as though there were no tomorrow. "These taste great. The guys are making fast work of the half-ton of meat the cook mentioned having smoked today."

She'd noticed how the Rebels' players treated Colin as though he were one of their own. "Your players all seem to like you."

He laughed. "They like me well enough until I start puttin' them to work. Seriously, my philosophy is pretty much that the team that plays together stays together—and not only on the field. Looks as though we're gonna get a show. A couple of these boys are good enough that they could make their living singing."

The DJ cranked up the karaoke machine, and three hulking linemen got up and belted out an old country-western classic, *Take It Easy*.

"They are good. Do you sometimes join them?" Susan thought he might—she couldn't imagine there being much of anything Colin didn't do well.

He grinned. "Once in a while. Want me to sing to you, do you?"

"I'd love to hear you, but only if you want to." She couldn't help imagining Colin's singing voice would sound even sexier than when he talked.

"Sure. Go grab one of the books and pick out whatever you'd like to hear, as long as it's country-western. I do a lousy job with rap and disco." He reached over, gave her a quick, hard kiss then shot her an evil grin. "If you pick out something embarrassing, I'm gonna make you pay."

She doubted she'd mind anything he'd do to her. After all, he wasn't likely to throw her on top of the table and fuck her brains out in front of people who might not be into domination and submission. Not to mention that children were present. Smiling at her selection, she hurried back to the table. "I gave Charley your name and the number of the song I'd like you to sing."

"Charley?"

"He's the guy who runs the karaoke machine."

When Colin grabbed her hand and laid it on his thigh she glanced around, wondering if anybody noticed. If they did, they weren't showing any reaction. Susan knew none of the locals would expect her to act shy. Besides, she didn't mind everybody knowing she and Colin were together. She needed to learn not to reserve even the slightest intimacy for the bedroom. Obviously Colin had no qualms about letting his sexual appetite show. It didn't matter now that Donnie had wanted to keep their bedroom games just between them—at least just between them and whatever man he decided to share her with at any given time. Tentatively, she laid her hand over Colin's, squeezed it.

He looked down at her, amusement in his gaze. "Easy, my little pet. All I'm doing now is staking my claim. Lettin' my players know you're mine just in case some of them get the idea they'd like a taste. What's this song you want to hear?"

When she told him he grinned. "Good. I like that one." When Charley called his name, he got up and pulled her along with him, seating her on a bar stool next to the microphone.

The café's single strobe light came on, bathing them in dappled shades of blue and yellow, the colors of the Hedgecock teams for as long as Susan could remember. It lent a surreal effect to the otherwise mundane gathering spot for Hedgecock locals, past and present. A short intro to the song she'd selected added to the temporary transformation, but then Colin began to sing. His deep, mellow voice surrounded her, took her to a world where there were only the two of them, an island apart within the packed café.

He held her gaze as he sang about making love, caring. Wanting more than an affair. Words she'd heard before in the old country-western song but until now had never really listened to, only let the tune carry her along. Words whose message now came through loud and clear. What she wanted. What he indulged her with, at least for now.

When the song was finished he grasped her at the waist and lifted her high above his head, his motion seemingly effortless. He let her down slowly, brushing her body against his. His arms encircled her once her feet hit the ground, and he bent and kissed her. He tasted good—sweet and spicy and ever so arousing when he slid his tongue between her lips and explored her mouth. She raised her arms and laid her hands on his broad, muscular shoulders.

The heat of his hard, fit body and his arms that held her as efficiently as cuffs or scarves set her heart to pounding. Her panties grew wet for the hard cock that branded her belly through the layers of their clothes. This afternoon he'd planted the seed in her mind, and now she imagined him taking her here, his pleasure enhanced by curious eyes—until he broke the kiss and herded her back to their table.

"I want you. I wish this were a sex club where folks wouldn't be scandalized if we put on a show." His tone was hard, as hard as his jeans-clad cock where he'd just placed her hand.

She'd never been fucked in front of witnesses who weren't participants, but the idea made her pussy clench with anticipation. Anticipation for what had always been forbidden, for the rush she imagined would come if she knew curious eyes were on her and Colin when he took her. "I wish that, too, Master."

"It will happen someday soon, pet. Count on it. Meanwhile, pretend I've got you on my lap, my cock buried deep in your wet, hot cunt. Your skirt will be draped over me so nobody can see us. But they'll know. They'll see you breathing hard and they'll notice how my jaw's clenched with the need to hold back. They'll smell sex all around us. They'll be able to tell you're on the edge because your nipples will be poking into that flimsy lace bra you're wearing, showing through your silky blouse."

His whispered words had her cunt on fire. "I'm wet for you already." The way his hard cock throbbed against her fingers told her his words had aroused him, too.

"That does it," he said, his expression fierce. "Get up. Stand in front of me and head for the first dark, deserted spot outside, next to a tree or building."

Susan obeyed, hoping her cheeks weren't as red as they felt when she made her way to the café door, Colin right behind her. Once out of the light, he took her hand, dragged her toward a darkened alleyway between the café and a deserted storefront next door. He paused for a minute then chose a spot against the store's weathered wall and pressed her hard against it. "I've gotta have my Susan fix."

"I'm glad."

"I'm glad you wore a dress tonight." Colin wasted no time gathering the material in his hands and hiking her skirt up. "And that this thong's easy to move out of my way." He inserted a long finger in her wet cunt, groaned. "God, I love how you're always wet for me. Unfasten my pants."

She fumbled with the zipper but got it undone and freed his rock-hard erection. "Seems you're ready, too."

"Yeah. I don't have a condom with me. Are you okay with that?"

She should have said no. But she was clean and she was sure he was, too. "Yes, Master. I could get pregnant, though."

His dark eyes glistened in the low light of a new moon. "If that happens we'll just have to deal with it. Together. Right now I'm gonna fuck you up against this wall. Put your legs around my waist and hold onto my shoulders." When she did, he braced her ass against the wall and impaled her—one smooth thrust that embedded his long, thick cock all the way inside her needy cunt. "God yeah."

His long fingers dug into her butt cheeks, holding her steady for his jackhammer-like pounding. The wet, slapping sounds of flesh on flesh filled the alleyway. Layers of denim abraded her slit, a reminder that they were doing this out where anybody could wander by and get an eyeful. No time for anything but his cock in her cunt, a furtive claiming that couldn't wait for a more private time.

She loved Colin. Loved everything about her Master—his strength but most of all his ability to meet her deepest needs that had gone unsatisfied so long. "Oh God, Master, may I come?"

"Yeah, baby." He tensed, slammed into her again. As her climax claimed her, she felt his hot semen start to spurt deep inside her. "Oh, yeah. Come for me now."

She loved the way he held her, as though he cherished her not just as a receptacle for his lust. Though she hated leaving him she slid her legs down and balanced on tiptoe, though he still held her securely in his arms.

* * * * *

They hadn't been back inside five minutes when huge all-pro defensive end Jimmy Bronson came over and stopped behind Susan's chair. Colin wanted nothing more than to tell the kid to get lost. But he couldn't. Jimmy, just traded to the Rebels a month ago, hadn't had to volunteer to assist at the football camp—he'd wanted to help out.

"Mind if I dance with your lady, Coach?"

Colin did, but he grinned and stood. He'd never noticed before how Jimmy towered over him, or how the kid's baby face contrasted with his thick neck and hulking body. "Susan, this is Jimmy Bronson. Make his day and join him for a spin around the dance floor. Jimmy, don't trample Susan."

"All right." She didn't sound overly enthusiastic when she got up and offered Jimmy her hand. When she smiled up at her dance partner, though, Colin felt a pang of jealousy he hadn't experienced for years, if ever.

It was worse because Colin had seen Jimmy playing at the club. The guy might be just twenty-six, but he already was an experienced Dom. A lifestyle sort, not just an occasional player in the BDSM games so many Rebels' players and coaches enjoyed to let off built-up frustrations. A couple of weeks ago Colin had jerked off while watching Jimmy play out a public scene with one of the club's more adventurous submissives.

The big kid was as dominant as any Master Colin had ever observed. He'd had the submissive moaning with ecstasy from all-over wax play. Apparently playing with wax was Jimmy's personal fetish. *Susan's into hot wax, too, damn it.* Colin and a half-dozen other club members had watched Jimmy wax and depilate every inch of the sub's body, leaving her oiled and gleaming as she squirmed on a fucking table, her arms and legs securely bound. Jimmy had fucked her to a huge orgasm then released her bonds. When she'd gone to her knees and begged him for more, he'd made her swallow his dick and begun methodically clipping away her short brown hair until nothing but stubble remained, while she gave him head.

While she'd kept on sucking his cock, Jimmy had dripped molten wax evenly all over her skull, rubbing it until it formed a hard cap then peeling it away and coming all over her gleaming, tattooed scalp.

No doubt Jimmy would enjoy waxing Susan's rose tattoo. No he wouldn't, because he'd never see it. Colin dug his fingernails into his palms so hard he wondered why he didn't draw blood when he watched the young Dom bend and whisper something in Susan's ear.

Thankfully the song ended and Jimmy brought Susan back to Colin. "Thanks, Coach," he said with an easy grin. "You've got a pretty lady here. Better take good care of her."

"I will." When a slow, sensual song began to play, Colin drew Susan to her feet and out to the dance floor. Their bodies moved in perfect synch, and her cheek felt right against his chest. While his players, his fellow quarterbacks and the Hedgecock locals looked on, Colin was falling not just in lust but in love with his submissive lover.

He didn't want to let her go when the last bars of the song played out, so he didn't. Lifting her into his arms, he strode out the café's swinging doors into the starry night.

"What?" She looked up at him, a surprised expression but no censure in her eyes.

"I'm taking you home. Don't feel like sharing you anymore tonight. The next few days we'll both be tied up with the football camp and the other festivities."

Chapter Four

ॐ

Hedgecock had taken on a carnival-like atmosphere, the smells of ribs and hot dogs and buttered popcorn pervading the air around the football field and school grounds. Colin missed Susan, who was tied up with Mel collecting fees for the camp and making sure everybody was where they needed to be.

Not that he wasn't busy. Over two hundred kids between twelve and eighteen were doing the camp. Some of them had promise. Others didn't, but they all seemed to be having fun. All except one little guy whose lower lip was quivering when he came up to Colin the last day of the camp, tears in his eyes.

"What's the matter, son?" Colin motioned to a wooden bench nearby. "Why don't we sit a minute and you tell me." He sat beside the kid, then took a long swallow of Gatorade.

"My dad says I have to learn to throw. He says that's the only way I'll ever get on a team, as scrawny as I am."

Colin would have enjoyed wrapping his hands around the neck of the kid's old man and squeezing until his eyes bugged out. "Well, I don't know about that, but if you want to learn to throw a football, you've come to the right place. There are four of us here, ready to teach you whatever you want to learn."

"You're all right-handed."

"So?"

"I'm a lefty."

Colin glanced at the boy's name tag. "Well, Todd, I'm right-handed, but I can throw pretty well with my left arm. I even did it once in a while in games back when I was playing in New York." He wouldn't mention that the only time he ever turned temporary southpaw was when a defender had a firm grip on his right arm. "Come on, let's give it a shot."

For the next hour Todd worked with Colin. The boy's hands were small, but he managed to hold the ball and throw some decent spirals once he got over being afraid of the ball. Not that Colin thought Todd had a future in the NFL, or even in a halfway competitive high school program, but his father hadn't needed to make the kid feel bad.

Colin would never make his own son feel unworthy—if he had one, that is. His mind drifted to Susan, to their unprotected lovemaking three nights ago, and he wondered...

It surprised the hell out of him that he halfway hoped she was. Maybe more than halfway. Colin had found the past few days that he enjoyed working with kids younger than the pros he'd been coaching since he gave up playing. He'd also learned he was happiest when he came home to a submissive lover, when his most pressing need was to ensure her pleasure.

He finished off his Gatorade and strode toward the registration booth. Toward Susan.

* * * * *

"Thanks for helping me, Coach," Todd said when he came up to Colin and Susan on the makeshift midway later after the camp was over. "I want you to meet my dad."

When he felt Susan's muscles tense up beneath his hand he slid his left arm around her waist more securely. He didn't like the vibes she was sending out, but he pasted on a smile and stuck out his free hand. "I'm Colin Zanardi. I enjoyed working with Todd today. You've got a good boy there."

The man's gaze was fixed not on Colin but on Susan. "Yeah. Guess it takes a big-shot, ex-NFL star to score with Ms. Anderson. Once he's gone maybe she'll start samplin' the local guys some more."

"That's enough." Colin wished to hell the asshole's son weren't right there soaking up the filthy accusations coming out of the guy's tobacco-stained mouth. "Todd, Ms. Anderson and I have to be going. You keep on practicing your throwing." Holding Susan firmly, he turned to walk away.

"Smart-ass sonofabitch. Might know he'd take up with the town whore."

Colin whirled around when he heard the bastard spouting such filth, and in front of his own kid. "I'd shut my filthy mouth if I were you," he snarled, fingers curled tightly into fists as he took a determined stride toward the disgusting creep. "If you don't, I'll shut it for you, here and now."

"Colin, please." Susan's soft hand on his forearm drew his attention, made him realize they were attracting a crowd. "He's not worth it."

She obviously wanted him to avoid making a scene. Colin nailed the guy with the most evil stare he could manage. "You heard the lady. She doesn't think you're worth me dirtying my hands on. I may decide she's wrong if I see your ugly face again, so I suggest you make yourself scarce."

"Thank you," she said quietly as they made a beeline for his car that he'd left by the field that morning.

Too quietly. Colin held a tight rein on the fury that made him want to tear that scruffy cowboy limb from limb. His concern now was for Susan. It was as though that worthless bastard had drained her of the vibrant love for life he'd felt in her since arriving on her doorstep five days ago.

When he slid behind the wheel he saw she was leaning against the passenger door, shoulders slumped. When she spoke, her voice was tiny, hesitant. "I should have known somebody would say something, but I can't imagine anybody but Virgil Lane talking that way in front of his own child."

Hurt. The motherfucker had hurt Susan. Colin had come to care for her, for much more than the fact that she made him feel ten feet tall and thirty again when they made love. "I'll get

Virgil away from Todd and then I'll shove his filthy tongue down his throat. Nobody's getting away with insulting you."

"They've been doing it a long time, with reason I guess. Since I wasn't terribly particular after Donnie died, the ones I turned down—like him—turned on me. Not that I'd have taken up with any guy who was married, even if he weren't disgusting like Virgil Lane." She choked back what sounded like a muffled sob. "I'm so sorry. I should have warned you somebody would say something like that."

It ate at Colin's gut to see Susan so torn. "You were right, sweetheart, when you said the jerk wasn't worth fighting. He's not worth a single tear out of your beautiful eyes, either. Give me a kiss now, and I'll take you home. Bet I can love you so good you'll forget all about old Virgil and his foul mouth."

Chapter Five

സ

She loved him. How on earth was she going to survive once Colin drove away tomorrow after the final ceremony was over? She'd let him undress them both and lead her into the small shower. Now she stood in his arms, water sluicing over their sweaty bodies. Water washing away the hurtful memory of Virgil Lane's insult—at least for now. Or so it was supposed to be doing.

Unfortunately the dirty words didn't disappear with the soapy water that was trickling down the drain. She couldn't help trembling, realizing this wonderful interlude with Colin, where she'd finally found her Master, would soon come to an end, leaving her where she'd been before, seeking something she wasn't likely to find again.

Donnie had been a hard act to follow. Susan didn't need a rocket scientist to tell her Colin might be damn near impossible to replace. Might? She chided herself on that one because she couldn't imagine there being a man on Earth who could replace him in her heart and mind. Trying to control an overwhelming sense of impending loss, she lathered her hands and soaped his muscular chest again.

Colin took her hand, drew it down to his half-hard penis. "You're supposed to be thinking about me. About this."

"Yes, Master." She loved touching him, feeling him grow bigger and harder under her seeking fingers. "You feel so good. I'll hate it when you're gone."

"Don't think about that. Just get on your knees and show me how much you like taking my cock down your pretty throat. I knew the first time I saw you that your mouth's made for sucking me."

Sucking me. Not sucking just any cock. "Yes, Master," she said, kneeling at his feet and drawing the purplish cock head between her lips. At his deep growl of approval she bathed him with her tongue, taking her time as she enjoyed the velvety texture of his flesh, the contrast of it with the cool, smooth ring that protruded from the slit at its tip.

He ran his calloused fingers through the wet strands of her hair, his touch reminding her he was in control. Arousing her as much as the act of giving him head, paying homage to his maleness. His mastery. "Sweetheart, I love the way you take care of me."

It took both her hands to enclose his long, thick shaft. "Yeah, like that." He arched his hips, fucked her mouth slowly, with shallow thrusts that only made her want more. Then he pulled away.

"I'm sorry, Master…"

He drew her to her feet, took her mouth in a hard, arousing kiss then wrapped both arms around her, his big hands pressing their bodies so close she gasped for breath.

"Don't be sorry. I find I want to touch you all over. Hold you. Can't do that with you on your knees playing with my cock. Let's dry off and go to bed."

* * * * *

She lay naked on the bed, beautifully submissive. But Colin didn't like seeing the sadness in her eyes when he dropped the towel and straddled her slender hips. "Get that bastard out of your head. If you can't I swear I'll go find him and make sure he never insults you again."

"I'm not thinking of that."

"Then what? I don't want you thinking about anything but me. Us. How great it's gonna feel when I fill your sweet cunt with my cock and fuck you until we both shatter in a thousand pieces." He bent, kissed first one nipple then the other.

"Oh, yes. Please."

"Please what?"

"Fuck me now. I want all the memories to hold me when you're gone."

Colin had expected from the first time they'd talked on the phone that he'd want Susan sexually. He hadn't thought until they'd spent this time together that he'd want to tear any man who insulted her limb from limb, or that he'd be thinking about a future with her, not only as his sex slave but also as his best friend and lover.

Closing his eyes against the bright afternoon sun streaming in the window, he played with her nipples, loving the way they hardened and elongated beneath his fingers. "I think I'll get you some rings so I can tug on them with my teeth and hook them together with a chain so I can drag you around whenever I feel like it."

The barbells frustrated him, mostly, he figured, because he hadn't personally inserted them into the neatly done horizontal piercings. "How would you like that?"

"Mmmm, I like that idea, Master." She snuggled closer, until her baby-smooth pussy brushed his erection.

He laid a hand on her mound. "This tattoo will have to go."

Looking up at him as he traced the faded mark put there by her first Master, she started to protest then closed her pretty lips.

"I'm thinking I want to be your Master, not just a week-long fuck partner. What do you think of that?"

She looked surprised—maybe even shocked. "You have to go back to work. Of course you could come back when you've got time. Like Dave and Keith and Bobby."

"Or you could just crawl in my car and go back to Savannah with me. Come to think of it, we could come back here to visit once in a while if that would make you happy." Colin didn't have the feeling of home that the other quarterbacks shared about their hometown. They all had relatives—or in Dave's case memories of his late grandma who'd raised him—to keep them connected in some way to what Colin only considered a place where he'd spent three years bridging from a happy childhood with his mom and stepfather to adulthood with only tenuous family ties to his nomadic father. "Do you have family here that you couldn't bear to leave?"

"No, Master. If I move away from this house, though, I lose the income from a trust Donnie left to take care of me. If I leave, the trust fund gets split between his kids. I can't imagine the few skills I have would be worth much. I didn't go to college or technical school. Donnie wanted me home for him 24/7."

The dead Donnie Anderson sounded like a prime SOB in addition to an old-style, lifestyle Dom. "Walk away from it. I'll take care of you. If you'd like, you could take college courses in Savannah. It's obvious you've got some real savvy about graphic art, from the program you put together for this reunion."

He hated that fucking tattoo. Taking his hand off it, he met Susan's confused gaze. "I'm gonna have this rosebud removed. Better yet, I'll have it covered with a new tattoo that will mark you as mine." He could hardly wait to find a reputable tattoo artist to wipe away the evidence of the Dom who'd put it there.

Maybe… "I may have your clit pierced, too, so it will match my cock." He slid his hand a little lower, found her rigid little button and scissored it between his fingers. "What would you think about that?"

"I'd love it." She shifted, giving him full access to her sex. "I'm not sure you could manage all these changes in just one day," she said, a tear making its way down her smooth, sun-kissed cheek.

Apparently he hadn't made himself clear. "As far as I'm concerned, we've got a lifetime. All you have to do is call whoever administers that trust and tell him to get the papers drawn up to give whatever's in it to Donnie's obnoxious kids." He paused for a minute, wondered if his precious submissive still had the capacity to trust after how her husband had left her as dependent as she'd been when he was alive. "I want you in my house, in my bed, in my life, 24/7. I don't expect to be your only interest, though. And I promise to take care of you so that if anything happens to me, you'll be free to go on with your life however you choose."

"You want me to be your full-time slave?" She sounded incredulous, but her smile lit up her face and warmed his heart.

"Yeah. I've been thinking about it since our first night together." He returned her smile then bent and kissed away the tears that welled in her eyes. "Are you ready to be my pet? My 24/7 slave?"

"I've been ready a long time. Ready to give my Master total control." Her eyes shone when she met his gaze. "I'm ready to belong to you for as long as you want me."

He splayed his fingers over her flat belly. "Okay. As soon as we finish here, I want you to get hold of whoever holds that trust and sign the papers to give it up."

"That would be Cal Tate. Donnie set the trust up at his bank."

"Good. I was worried we might have to drive a bit to get that handled. Starting today, I'll take care of you financially."

"I'll hate that. I've liked being able to take care of myself since Donnie died." Her little frown made Colin feel guilty.

"With his money."

"Yes, but—"

"But nothing. I take care of my woman. Not that I plan to keep you chained to my bed. You'll have an account to take care of the condo, yourself and me. You can shop to your heart's content while I'm working. Speaking of shopping, I'll insist on it. It makes me feel good to see my slave in pretty clothes and jewelry that will make my friends jealous. Any objections?"

"N-no. You must have some rules, though." Her mouth puckered a little, as though she were half serious, half joking.

He figured he'd better take her seriously. "Just a few, sweetheart. First off, you're mine. All mine unless I choose to share you in a scene some time." At the moment he couldn't envision letting any other man or woman touch what he'd claimed as his, but he had to allow that it might someday happen.

"All right. That's easy." From the solemn look in her dark eyes, he didn't doubt she meant that quick response, though he might have, knowing she'd entertained a lot of cocks since her old Master had died, by her own admission.

"Next, you're my responsibility and my pleasure. You'll trust me to take care of you not just sexually but in everything." He couldn't wait to see her in finery he'd buy her, feel silk and lace sliding against his naked body whenever he took her. "You'll leave here and go with me, but you'll take nothing but what you're wearing. I don't want you having things somebody else bought for you."

As though she understood why he was making this condition, she looked over at him and nodded. "Anything else, Master?"

"You'll keep your pussy shaved smooth and ready for me any time, any place. If I want to make love with you someplace where we might be seen or even with others present, you won't object." At her questioning look, he said, "We all have our little fetishes. You seem to get off on being restrained. Not to mention wax play, which we'll do at my club in Savannah where all the necessary precautions are handy. I'm a bit of a voyeur, myself. I find it incredibly exciting, watching people fuck…and having others watch me. Not that I seem to need any extra stimulation when I'm making love with you."

"Oh." She stroked his chest, drawing circles around his nipples before lowering her hand to encircle his engorged cock. "I think I might like watching, too. And when you're touching me, I don't think I'd even notice if we were providing a show for somebody else. What else, Master?"

"For now, I think that takes care of everything. Is there anything you want from me? Other than for me to be your Master?"

She looked into his eyes, smiled. "I'd like to have your baby. If you don't mind."

Did he mind? Colin didn't know. But he recalled having the fleeting thought earlier in the week that he'd like to make her pregnant. And he'd felt a twinge of envy for Keith when he'd watched the younger man look at his little boy with so much love. "You don't think I'm too old to be a dad?"

"No more than I'm too old to be thinking about babies when I could have one old enough to be in college. But…"

"Why didn't you and your husband have kids?"

Susan shook her head. "He didn't want any. His own sons were grown and gone before he married me. Besides, he'd had a vasectomy before the younger one was born."

Colin didn't like to see her dark eyes cloud with apparent regret. It pissed him off that the old Dom had taken a young girl and basically treated her like another child, only with bedroom privileges. "Do you see his kids?"

"No. I never met either of them until Donnie's funeral. They seemed to think they should have shared in whatever Donnie had. I gave them most of the money but kept this house and the income from a trust fund he'd set up for all of us. I haven't heard from either boy since."

"Assholes." As much as he'd have liked to rant and rave about her late husband and the swine who'd wanted nothing from Susan but what they considered their share of their old man's leftovers, Colin said nothing. He just gathered Susan in his arms and held her for a long time, considering what she'd asked of him.

A child. He'd be seventy years old before the kid graduated from college. But his own dad was brimming with energy at seventy-five, still supervising drilling crews all over the South. Several NFL coaches were pushing seventy, too — they didn't seem to have slowed down. Maybe fifty was the new thirty, as some pundits loved to say.

Colin couldn't honestly say he'd be too old to take his son or daughter to Little League. After all, he made his living working with pro athletes. Surely he could coach Pee Wee football without any problems. He slid his fingers through Susan's silky hair, loved the feel of it. The feel of her. Then he tilted her head, met her gaze.

"If we can, we'll make a baby. If not, we can adopt. Of course we'll get married before any baby comes along. I think you'll be a good mother, and though it's a pretty late date for me to make a decision like this, I believe I'd like to be a dad." He watched her beautiful eyes tear up, as though he'd given her a wonderful gift. "I get the idea that's okay with you. Right?" He used his thumb to wipe away the moisture from her cheeks.

She sniffled, but the smile she gave him lit up his heart. "It's more than okay. I thought this morning when I was watching Keith's little boy playing how I'd love to have a child with you — before it's too late."

Blood rushed to his sex, leaving him feeling lightheaded. He laid a hand on her flat abdomen, splayed his fingers over the smooth, soft flesh. "Do you have any idea how hot it makes me, imagining your belly getting round with my baby?"

"It makes me hot, too. Hot and very, very wet." Her legs opened in obvious, exquisite invitation.

Not about to say no, he rolled her onto her back, settled between her legs. "What say we start on this project right now?" he asked as he rubbed his swollen cock along her wet, warm slit. "No condom. Missionary position. No kink that might embarrass that little egg and sperm and keep them from getting it on."

She laughed then laid small kisses along his shoulder and throat. "You're silly. But I love…it."

Did she love him? He hoped so though he wasn't ready to call his feelings for her love. Lust for a lifetime of her submission? Sure. That was a no-brainer. He rubbed the tip of his cock along her wet, inviting slit, savoring the feel of naked flesh rubbing naked flesh. "I'd almost forgotten until the other night outside the café, how much my cock hates wearing a raincoat. Your little pussy feels so hot, so wet."

She squirmed a little, as though impatient for him to claim her. "Fuck me, Master. Please."

He pressed inside her until his cock head lay just inside her wet, swollen labia, felt her pulsating around him. Her sensual heat bathed him, made him crazy to bury himself. "So warm and welcoming." Slow and deep, he sank all the way to the mouth of her womb then slid out again. Over and over, claiming her as he'd never claimed a lover before. Smooth and sweet, vanilla with the promise of something more. Something better than fresh strawberries piled on top of the ice cream to add a little bright, sweet flavor.

She cupped his face in her soft hands and placed little kisses on his lips, his chin. When she met his gaze her eyes shone brightly. "This feels like making love should feel."

"Yeah, it does." He was in no hurry. Her little moans were music in his ears, welcome punctuation to the sounds and heady smells of sex. He bent, took her mouth, caught her little scream of pleasure as her cunt convulsed around him and she tightened her legs around his waist. He was close. Raising himself on his outstretched arms, he looked down at them, watched his cock disappear into her spasming cunt then reappear, slick and wet with her juices. "Look at us, baby. Omigod!"

He couldn't hold back. Had to come. Couldn't talk. Couldn't think, only feel. Her tight, wet cunt milked his cock. He let go, spurt after hard spurt of hot semen against the mouth of her womb.

"Oh, yes, Master..."

She convulsed around him, greedily milking the last drop of his climax. He loved it, loved the feeling of completion he'd been missing so long. Maybe forever. "Oh, yeah, indeed." When he rolled with her onto his side, he didn't withdraw but stayed inside her, savoring the little aftershocks that flowed from her pussy to his own spent flesh.

It had taken years and come in the most improbable of places, but Colin knew for sure, his cock had finally found its home.

* * * * *

The following afternoon, Mel Tate stood with Susan, their job of handling receipts and expenditures finally finished. "Why don't you go on out toward the field and watch the contest? I know you're dying to see him throw."

Cal had to have told her, but Susan didn't care. She fingered the gold medallion Colin had put around her neck this morning, promising a real collar as soon as he could get to a proper store. "Yeah, Mel, I want to watch. My bet's on Colin to show up the other guys."

"Is it true you're leaving with him?"

Susan wondered how long it would take for her to quit pinching herself every time she thought about her new Master taking her with him. "Yes, it's true." Susan imagined a lot of the women in Hedgecock would be meowing like cats in heat when they heard the news — some of the men, too. But Mel had befriended her last fall when they'd first started planning this reunion, and Susan felt sure the other woman wished her well. "We'll be leaving tonight, as soon as this is over."

"Come on, then, you don't want to miss this." Grabbing Susan's hand, Mel tugged her out by the bleachers, where a huge crowd had gathered to watch Colin and the others. Several Rebels' players had gone on the field, their assignments to catch passes for the quarterbacks.

Colin looked great. He'd surprised her that morning by pulling out shorts and a jersey from the New York team where he'd quarterbacked for so many years. "Can't wear Rebels gear and steal Dave's thunder," he'd told her. "Besides, I need to match your program, don't I?"

Now he was on the field with the other three homegrown heroes, his royal blue and white jersey standing out vividly among the rainbow of team colors. Susan held her breath while they all did a few warm-up throws. "I hear congratulations are in order," Diane said, and Susan smiled and thanked her.

She thought the other woman meant her good wishes, and she was sure Keith Connors' young wife was thrilled that another Hedgecock quarterback had found his match there. Marly Anthony practically burst into a cheer when she came up to add her congratulations just as the contest was beginning.

The crowd roared. It seemed each spectator had his or her favorite. Bobby went first, then Dave. Colin followed and Keith brought up the rear. Cal had devised a complicated scoring system based on number of yards thrown and the accuracy of throws aimed at barrel staves.

Susan's eyes were glued on Colin, or rather on the back of the blue jersey with "Zanardi" and a big white number eight trimmed in red. For a minute she wished she'd met him back when he'd been playing, but then she remembered Elise—and her own first Master.

Their time was now. It hadn't been twenty years ago. She let out a huge cheer when Colin arrowed a perfect spiral through the barrel stave from half the length of the field. He was so good her heart nearly burst with pride. She sat on the folding chair she'd dragged along, watched the competition that seemed so close—too close to call by her count. He made the same perfect throw from sixty yards, came up a little short from seventy. Bobby's last throw had gone the distance but barely missed the target. Dave's had been short, too, not that anybody expected him to make all the long ones since his heavily braced knee kept him from getting his body fully behind the throws.

Susan watched Keith get set for his final throw. This year's Super Bowl MVP, the lanky quarterback was good. Damn good. She held her breath as his perfect spiral zoomed toward the target—held on a lucky gust of wind—and fell just short of the barrel stave and landed next to the last ball Colin had thrown.

All four men stood on the field, enjoying what looked like a pleasant conversation while Cal tallied up the scores. When he came up on the risers and grabbed the microphone, Susan crossed her fingers and kept her gaze glued on Colin's gorgeous face. He'd said it didn't matter, the contest was just for fun. But she knew it did. Like all the Hedgecock quarterbacks, he had an ego she knew needed regular feeding.

Cal called out for everybody's attention. Susan saw Marly draw in a deep breath. Tina dropped her gaze to little Jack while Diane fiddled with the braided leash attached to Dave's sooty standard poodle. The dog had wanted badly to go on the field and join the fun. In spite of telling herself this was all in good fun, Susan felt her heart pounding.

Then Cal made the announcement. Colin and Keith had tied, with Dave and Bobby coming in only a point or two behind. "Let's have a big hand for all four of these guys who came back and made this reunion a huge success."

Cal announced the numbers Susan and Mel had calculated—an amount that should take care of the most needed renovations. Then he called Colin to the risers and handed him the microphone.

Colin laid an envelope in Cal's hand. "The other guys asked me to speak for all of us, so here I am, feeling great and none the worse for wear after coming back to the field where I got my start in football over thirty years ago. Bobby, Keith, Dave and I all want to give back to Coach Williams and his program that gave us the basics before we went off to college and the NFL. Cal, we hope the school board will use these checks from us to further sports at Hedgecock High."

Colin looked around, found Susan and motioned her to join him. "Aside from getting the start of my long career as a player and coach in the NFL, I need to thank Hedgecock for bringing me here to find the woman I've been looking for longer than I like admitting. I knew from the first time I heard Susan's soft, slow drawl when she called to ask me to come that she'd be a very special lady and she is. I'm taking her home with me, but I promise to bring her back next year so we can both take part in the second annual Hedgecock football camp."

His dark eyes sparkled and his smile took her breath away when he held both her hands and brushed his chiseled lips across hers. "Now it's time for us to go, folks. Until next year."

Epilogue
Savannah, Georgia, four months later
ഔ

"How's my baby doing?" Colin shucked his suit jacket and loosened his tie as soon as he set Susan on the carpeted floor of their bedroom. The party they'd thrown had been fun but now he wanted nothing more than to make love for the first time with his brand new bride.

Her smile warmed his heart and sent blood rushing to his cock. "He's fine. And so am I." She looked down at the diamond-studded band he'd slid next to the five-carat solitaire he'd bought the first chance he got after they left Hedgecock. "Your dad's a lot like you."

"Yeah. I hope I'm in as good shape as Zeke is when I hit seventy-five. He told me I'd done good this time, you know." Colin had already known that, of course, but it hadn't hurt to hear the words from his dad. "He even promised to come when Bruiser's born since neither of us has any other relatives to help out."

Since they'd been together, Colin had pieced together Susan's history, which she still found so hard to talk about—the strict great-aunt who'd raised her until her death, her typical teenage rebellion against rules so strict they practically ensured rebellion and the loneliness and need for an older mentor that had practically shoved her into Donnie Anderson's arms.

Colin held her, gently working the buttons loose at the back of the violet silk halter dress she'd picked to wear for their wedding because she thought its high waist concealed her growing baby bump. "Are you happy, sweetheart?"

"Delirious. I could hardly believe so many Hedgecock people came. Even Diane was all smiles. Guess she's forgiven me now that she's so sure Dave's all hers."

"They all love you now, sweetheart, because they realize you've made me the happiest man alive." Truth was, Colin had been surprised but very pleased to see Mel and Cal—and all three of his fellow quarterbacks who'd formed friendships that crossed generations but were glued together by a shared love for the game. "Come here."

She did. He'd known she would because his wishes were always her commands. Very gently he lifted the gown off her body and bent to nuzzle her belly, now minus the navel ring she'd removed as soon as they'd found out about the baby. "Lie down."

Eagerly, she obeyed his softly spoken order, her ripening body fascinating him more every day. The adoring way she watched him strip off his clothes made him feel ten feet tall, as powerful as he'd ever felt. "I'm gonna tie you up and have my wicked way with you."

"Promises, promises, my darling Master." When she stretched out her arms and legs, he couldn't help noticing her new tattoo—the exotic-looking, soft lavender orchid on her mound. He'd chosen it as soon as they'd gotten back from Hedgecock, his personal brand to replace the rose from the past he swore he'd make her forget. "Make love with me, Master. Please."

Very gently he bound her to the bed the way he'd done that first night back in Hedgecock. Then, starting with her lush mouth, he claimed her body as she'd taken his heart. Gently, gradually, banishing his doubts, the disillusionment that had colored his life. Before Susan. "I love you, wife. I love our life and in a few months I'm gonna love our baby."

Slowly he made his way down her lush body, nibbling nipples made supersensitive by her pregnancy despite the fact she'd removed the nipple rings and put them away. Her little moans and sighs punctuated his every kiss as he made his way down her body, licking and kissing and nipping at her satiny skin.

Finally he knelt between her legs and sank into her wet heat. The way she clamped down on his cock made him feel strong, invincible. "Yeah, squeeze me like that. I'm not gonna last long." Then he felt a tiny flutter against his belly and looked into her shining eyes. "Was that..."

"Yes, Master, he's moving around."

"I hope I'm not hurting him."

She laughed, the sound surrounding him with emotion. "I think he's just saying hello to his daddy."

"Good." Colin sank into her again, slow and deep. Once, twice, three times as the pressure built in his balls...

And then she screamed with pleasure, and he filled her with his love.

Later he untied her and gathered her in his arms. "I'm a selfish bastard, sweetheart, but I don't believe I'll ever be able to share you, not even in a scene at Necessary Roughness."

"You're more than enough Master for me," she said sleepily, snuggling into his arms the way that made him feel like twice the man he was.

The End

Also by Ann Jacobs

Print Books:
A Mutal Gavor

A Shining Future

Another Love

Bound by Love

Controlled by Love

Black Gold: Dallas Heat

Enchained (*anthology*)

Eternally His

Firestorm

Forbidden Fantasies (*anthology*)

Full Circle

Haunted

Heart of the West

Lords of Pleasure

Out of Bounds

Sandstorms

The Defenders

The Prosecutors

About the Author

ℭ

Ann Jacobs is a sucker for lusty Alpha heroes and happy endings, which makes Ellora's Cave an ideal publisher for her work. Romantica®, to her, is the perfect combination of sex, sensuality, deep emotional involvement and lifelong commitment—the elusive fantasy women often dream about but seldom achieve.

First published in 1996, Jacobs has sold over forty books and novellas, some of which have earned awards including the Passionate Plume (best novella, 2006), the Desert Rose (best hot and spicy romance, 2004) and More Than Magic (best erotic romance, 2004). She has been a double finalist in separate categories of the EPPIES and From the Heart RWA Chapter's contest. Three of her books have been translated and sold in several European countries.

A CPA and former hospital financial manager, Jacobs now writes full-time, with the help of Mr. Blue, the family cat who sometimes likes to perch on the back of her desk chair and lend his sage advice. He sometimes even contributes a few random letters when he decides he wants to try out the keyboard. She loves to hear from readers, and to put faces with names at signings and conventions.

Ann Jacobs welcomes comments from readers. You can find her website and email address on her author bio page at www.ellorascave.com.

Tell Us What You Think

We appreciate hearing reader opinions about our books. You can email us at Comments@EllorasCave.com.

Why an electronic book?

We live in the Information Age—an exciting time in the history of human civilization, in which technology rules supreme and continues to progress in leaps and bounds every minute of every day. For a multitude of reasons, more and more avid literary fans are opting to purchase e-books instead of paper books. The question from those not yet initiated into the world of electronic reading is simply: *Why?*

1. *Price.* An electronic title at Ellora's Cave Publishing and Cerridwen Press runs anywhere from 40% to 75% less than the cover price of the exact same title in paperback format. Why? Basic mathematics and cost. It is less expensive to publish an e-book (no paper and printing, no warehousing and shipping) than it is to publish a paperback, so the savings are passed along to the consumer.

2. *Space.* Running out of room in your house for your books? That is one worry you will never have with electronic books. For a low one-time cost, you can purchase a handheld device specifically designed for e-reading. Many e-readers have large, convenient screens for viewing. Better yet, hundreds of titles can be stored within your new library—on a single microchip. There are a variety of e-readers from different manufacturers. You can also read e-books on your PC or laptop computer. (Please note that Ellora's Cave does not endorse any specific brands.

You can check our websites at www.ellorascave.com or www.cerridwenpress.com for information we make available to new consumers.)

3. *Mobility.* Because your new e-library consists of only a microchip within a small, easily transportable e-reader, your entire cache of books can be taken with you wherever you go.

4. *Personal Viewing Preferences.* Are the words you are currently reading too small? Too large? Too… ANNOYING? Paperback books cannot be modified according to personal preferences, but e-books can.

5. *Instant Gratification.* Is it the middle of the night and all the bookstores near you are closed? Are you tired of waiting days, sometimes weeks, for bookstores to ship the novels you bought? Ellora's Cave Publishing sells instantaneous downloads twenty-four hours a day, seven days a week, every day of the year. Our webstore is never closed. Our e-book delivery system is 100% automated, meaning your order is filled as soon as you pay for it.

Those are a few of the top reasons why electronic books are replacing paperbacks for many avid readers.

As always, Ellora's Cave and Cerridwen Press welcome your questions and comments. We invite you to email us at Comments@ellorascave.com or write to us directly at Ellora's Cave Publishing Inc., 1056 Home Avenue, Akron, OH 44310-3502.

ELLORA'S CAVE
Romanticon

Annual convention
for women who
refuse to behave

Discover for yourself why readers can't get enough
of the multiple award-winning publisher

Ellora's Cave.

Whether you prefer e-books or paperbacks,
be sure to visit EC on the web at
www.ellorascave.com

for an erotic reading experience that will leave you
breathless.

Made in the USA
Lexington, KY
29 November 2010